For Love of Charity

Wanda Parker

Published by:
Southern Yellow Pine (SYP) Publishing
4351 Natural Bridge Rd.
Tallahassee, FL 32305

www.syppublishing.com

This is a work of fiction. Names, characters, places, and events that occur either are the products of the author's imagination or are used fictitiously. Any resemblance to actual persons, places, or events is purely coincidental.

The contents and opinions expressed in this book do not necessarily reflect the views and opinions of Southern Yellow Pine Publishing, nor does the mention of brands or trade names constitute endorsement.

ISBN-10: 1-940869-70-6
ISBN-13: 978-1-940869-70-4
ISBN-13: ePub 978-1-940869-71-1
Library of Congress Control Number: 2016936261

Printed in the United States of America
First Edition
March 2016

Dedication

This is dedicated to all my Colonial Scots-Irish ancestors who fought their way into the wilderness to make homes and whose courage inspired this book. I also salute my Cherokee ancestors who liked their lives the way they were and wished the whites had stayed away

Acknowledgements

Thanks to my daughters, Kimberlie Parker and Katherine Parker-Egner, for reading, offering suggestions, and giving support, and encouragement while this book was incubating and finally hatching into a published work.

A special thanks to friends Jeanne Wehrmeyer, Linda Lanzarotta, and Nona Cody for their encouragement through the years.

Last but not least, thanks to Terri Gerrell of Southern Yellow Pine Publishing for taking a chance on me.

Chapter 1

Holding on to the splintery wooden rail, Charity climbed up stairs made of hewn logs. She stood outside the door, fighting the urge to throw up.

"A lady doesn't throw up in public," she mumbled, repeating what her mother once told her. "Nor does a lady keep going into places like this," she said to herself, taking another deep breath. "A place like this. Ha! This is one of the nicer places I've been to in the past few months. I hope this is almost over, and I find Robert inside. Then we can go back to civilization and have the wedding we planned."

Squaring her shoulders and stiffening her back, she walked into the dingy roadhouse with her head high. Unshaven, buckskin clad men nudged each other and stared at her as the hard wooden heels of her city shoes clicked across the uneven, split-log floor. Cheeks aflame, she looked around for the owner. A portly man wearing a soiled apron approached her.

Miss, you shouldn't be in a place like this," he said. "There's a nice inn just down the road. I can get someone to escort you there."

"Thank you, you're very kind," she answered, "but I'm already staying at that inn. Have you ever heard of Robert Larkin?"

"Robert Larkin?" he said, wrinkling his brow and scratching his nose. "Nooo, I can't say as I have."

Taking another deep breath, she bolstered her courage. "Then how about John Mason? I heard he was staying here so may I see him? It's very important that I talk to him."

"Yes miss, he was staying here until he ran out of money. Now, I think he's sleeping in the stable out back. Sit down and I'll send for him. It wouldn't be proper for a lady like you to go out there alone."

Sitting down at a rough table, Charity thought if the innkeeper knew what she intended to ask John Mason to do, he wouldn't think that proper, either. Ignoring the stares of the men, Charity dusted off the log bench and sat primly in the corner. She tried to look out the window, barely able to see through the wavy glass, dirt, and spider webs. All the houses were similar, built of heavy logs and weathered, with no apparent thought to property lines or directions. The chinking between the logs, needed so badly in the winter, was already pushed out for ventilation in the coming summer heat. How appropriate that the name of the roadhouse was Mud Flat.

Sitting by herself, she wondered what she was doing there alone. This was insane for her to attempt. *What would Mother and Father think if they were alive and saw me here? Well, for one thing, if they were alive, I wouldn't have to be here. Now, if I can get this man to take me to Robert, maybe my life can settle down without having to chase my future husband across mountain ranges. Then I can be a proper wife.*

While she waited, she thought back on the events that had brought her on this journey. Her parents owned a small farm that provided the family a modest living. They insisted Charity be raised proper so she would be able to marry well, educating her far better than most girls her age. Her manners and her clothing had to be spotless, and her father even taught her to handle finances and accounts.

The closest neighbors were the Larkins, owners of the largest plantation in the area. A motherless child, young Robert Larkin, liked to come over and spend time at Charity's house when they were young. He said her home was warm and inviting, whereas his was cold and impersonal since his mother died. With so few children in the area, she was his only friend, and they spent many hours dreaming of things to come when they grew up. Robert was going off on some adventure and considering a sail around the world. Charity was going to meet Prince Charming and live in a castle.

Charity's life was uneventful until her parents died in a carriage accident when she was thirteen. Her parents had ridden into town to get supplies for the party they were hosting for Mr. Larkin and Robert. When word came that an accident had taken the lives of both her parents, she was left in a void and filled with terror.

According to workers in the fields, something spooked the normally calm horses. They started an uncontrollable gallop, veering off into a deep ditch with no thought to the carriage they pulled behind them. Her parents had been tossed from the carriage like rag dolls, leaving her forever.

As she had no other relatives and he considered her part of the family, Mr. Larkin moved Charity into their palatial home, handled all of her legal affairs, and set up a trust for when she reached maturity.

Suddenly the Larkin house came to life with the sounds of two teenagers getting into mischief and running down the long halls, giggling at the latest prank they just played on the servants. With others to do the housework, Charity and Robert spent most of their time together studying the classics or playing the piano. Charity was able to help Robert, who struggled with his lessons, until even the tutor was pleased with his progress.

Mr. Larkin hinted many times over the years that he hoped she and Robert would marry when they reached eighteen. When the day approached, Charity, who was always fond of Robert, convinced herself she really loved him and began to plan the wedding.

Three months before the wedding, however, they woke to find Robert gone. He had packed a small valise, taken what money he had from his mother's inheritance and left home. He left no note, no explanation, nothing. Mr. Larkin's health seemed to deteriorate from that day on.

She began her search by questioning Robert's acquaintances, and that was where she first heard of John Mason. It appeared Robert had a partner and John Mason was a man she and her future father-in-law knew nothing about.

It took weeks of asking questions at frontier settlements to track down someone who knew how to find John Mason. Mostly, she got blank stares or disgusted looks at the mention of her search for two men who evidently didn't want to be found. She kept going from settlement to settlement, each one smaller than the last, until by a stroke of good fortune, she stumbled on Mud Flat. It was her first hint of luck. Grimy floors and judgmental stares were nothing to her now, if only John Mason would point her in the right direction.

Charity was embarrassed when her fiancé walked out so close to their wedding. She felt it strange, however, that she did not think of it as losing a fiancé, but as losing her best friend.

The wait seemed like hours. Ignoring the stares of the other customers, she waited patiently until the innkeeper re-entered. He was guiding a drunken man with one arm around the man's waist, holding the drunk's arm over his shoulder. He plopped the man down right across from her and the stout log table wobbled when his body bumped against it.

"Here he is, miss. I knew he was drinking, but I didn't expect him to still be this drunk. I'm sorry about this, but you did say it was important you speak to him, and I couldn't let you go talk to him in the stable. Get some coffee in him and maybe he'll sober up, but it may take a while. That rotgut he's been drinking would kill a mule."

Watching the man go limp, then start sliding slowly toward the table, her eyes widened. When his head slammed down on the hard wooden tabletop, his dirty, blond hair tumbled way too close to her, but the table held him in place.

Instinctively, she sprang back from him, taking out a dainty handkerchief which she held close to her nose. Unfortunately, it couldn't block the smell of alcohol, unwashed hair, horse manure, dirty straw, and chicken droppings spilling toward her. She muttered, "What am I doing in this situation?"

Just then, the innkeeper waddled up with a huge pot of coffee and two beer tankards and plopped them on the table in front of her.

"Here you go miss. I'll let you pour this down him. I gotta wait on my other customers."

"But…, but how am I supposed to get him to drink it when he's out cold?"

"Just lift him by his hair and pour," was the response as he walked back behind the bar to his customers.

"Fill him up til he pukes," said a man at another table. "That should sober him up. Say, ain't that the feller that's always trying to hire men to go into Cherokee territory with him? Stupid fool, I ain't crazy enough to get in the middle of them Injuns."

Charity's ears turned red and her cheeks flushed as the men called out. She fought the instinct to run, but she desperately needed information. Holding her breath, she slid next to the inebriated John Mason, and with shaking hands, she poured a liberal amount of coffee into one of the tankards. Grabbing a handful of his dank hair, she poured the scalding hot coffee into his half-open mouth.

"Holy Hell, I'm on fire!" he screamed, then his eyes rolled up and he passed out again.

Well, at least I had his attention for a little while, Charity thought with a smile.

She blew on the coffee to cool it, and begging and cajoling, she forced almost a whole gallon of coffee into him. When his eyes finally stayed open, he started gagging. Knowing what was coming, she moved quickly to get him outside, but his deadweight was more than she could handle.

Seeing her struggle, the innkeeper helped Charity get the man named John Mason to his feet and out the door. They got him outside just as the coffee shot out his mouth and nose. John held on to the rail and retched for several minutes amid laughter from onlookers crowding the door, watching his misery.

"Isn't there a gentleman among you who will help us?" she asked, hoping someone would take the hint.

"Mam, there ain't ary a gentleman around here," said one of the rough-looking men. "We're all just common hard working folk, but we'll help you with him if'n that's what you mean." A man with long hair and a beard walked over and put John's arm over his shoulder. "Where do you want him, miss?"

"Over by the well, if you please," she said with real gratitude. "Maybe some cold water will bring him around."

Together they helped John Mason to the well, sitting him beside the stone trough. Charity's helper drew water from the well, and using the gourd dipper hanging on the side, poured water over his head.

"There you go miss," her helper said. "I don't know what you want with him. But, now he's cleaner and a little more sober. Good day to you."

"My thanks for your help sir," Charity said, watching him leave with dismay. Now, she was left with a drunken, sodden, and barely coherent, John Mason, who was sitting in a mud hole in front of her. She sat still watching cautiously as he tried to focus on her, shaking his head occasionally. She figured he was trying to place her among the women he knew.

Suddenly, he shook his head hard, sending spray, bits of straw, and other stuff that had been clinging to his hair all over her. Then he grabbed his head in pain, saying, "Hey ladies, why'd jou make me shober up? Who are you three anyway?"

"My name is Charity," she said, thinking quickly. "My…, my husband is Robert Larkin. I've been told you are his partner, and you know where he is. I need your help to find him."

"Well, he ain't lost, sho…sho which one of you ladies need to find him?"

"Me. I'm trying to find him, Mr. Mason," she said with more force. "He's my husband so will you take me to him?"

Mason's eyes started to roll again when he hollered, "Hell no! I ain't takin' a helplessh woman out in the woods full of Injuns, wild animals, and sssuch. You wouldn't last a day out there, a del…, a deli…." He took a deep breath, "A delicate woman like you."

"I can pay you to take me to him."

"Pay me. Hail, you ain't got 'nough money," he paused, again trying to decide which of the women was speaking, "to pay me to…to…to…" His tongue seemed to stick to his teeth, and he started in the middle of a sentence. "…take you where few white men hasss ever been. There's danger all around." He swung his arm in a wide circle and nearly fell over. "Ever step of the way. Beshides, I don't think Robert wan's to be found." His energy depleted, he slumped back down.

"Why do you think that?" she asked, trying to keep her voice calm.

"I have my reasons," He tried to look mysterious, but he leaned too far to one side to keep it up for long.

"So, you hate Robert?"

"Who shaid I hate him? He's my partner and, an, my bestes fren'. Who shaid that? I'll whup the bastard." His eyes closed, and he leaned his head against the cool water trough. "Wife, Robert never mentioned he had a wife back home, and he never acted like he had one either."

"And yet you refuse to help me find him?" There was that cool, insistent voice again.

He sat with his eyes closed. Charity suspected he was wishing the pushy woman would go away and let him sober up in peace.

"We all have our reasons for doin' what we do. Jus' tell me what you want Robert to know, an, and when I see him, I'll tell him."

"No, Mr. Mason, I have to see him and talk to him myself," she said. "I must convince him to come home. I promised his father before he died that I would find Robert and…and bring him home. He can't waste his life out here in this God forsaken wilderness, living with heathens. He should be home where he belongs. Please help me. I'm not used to having to beg, but I'm begging you."

"Lady, I'm telling you for the las' time, I ain't takin' you nowheres. You wouldn't last a day carrying a heavy pack, and I don't have time to waste babying you all the way, what with Injuns and all. Beshides, it's indecent for you to even aash me.

Shame on you, a lady like you, wantin' to traipse off into the woods with me. Now, that's downright sscandalous. So, you go home, and if you wanna send a message to Robert, I'll take it to him. Now, 'scuse me, I gotta get ready to leave. Good day to you, miss, and good-bye."

Charity watched him rise painfully and stagger toward the livery stable. Resting her head against the cool rock of the well, she thought, *What a disagreeable man. But, he's my last hope to reach Robert. If he won't help me then I've failed to keep my promise to his father. Failed miserably!*

She watched Mason enter the livery stable to find the stable boy. She followed and stopped just outside the door to listen.

"Did you get word to your cousin? Is he goin' to be here afore dawn? I need to know he'll be here for sure since I want ta get an early shtart."

"Yes sir," said the boy, Charity saw his fingers crossed behind his back. "He promised he'd be here. He's anxious to earn the money you promised him if'n he carries a pack for you."

"None of the men aroun' here has 'nough guts to leave the clearing, let alone travel for hundreds of miles into Injun country. Jus' a bunch of gutless wonders all of 'em. I even off…offer—" he belched, "offered a bonus when we came back loaded with furs. Nooo takers. You sure your cousin is comin'? He's reliable, you say?" John sat on a pile of straw, holding his throbbing head.

"Yes sir, he'll be here." His hands back on his pitchfork, the boy watched Mason begin dividing his wrapped packets of trade goods into two piles.

Charity waited until John Mason finished dividing the packs and then lay down in the hay to sleep off his hangover. An outrageous plan formed in her mind that made more and more sense to her. What if, what if she went with him, not as a woman for sure, but what if she didn't appear to be a woman?

Walking over to the stable boy she softly asked, "Excuse me, I overheard you talking with Mr. Mason just now. May I ask you a question?" She watched Mason to make sure he couldn't hear their conversation.

"Yes miss, can I help you? Having never seen a well-dressed lady on this side of the settlement, he looked her up and down.

She fixed him with a steady stare and asked, "Is your cousin really going west with Mr. Mason?"

His face turned red, he glanced at Mason before giving Charity a sheepish grin and slowly shaking his head. "No miss, I ain't even got a cousin. I just told him that so he would stop pestering folks about going with him. I was going to make sure I wasn't anywhere around in the morning when he got ready to leave. Are you going to tell on me?"

"What's your name?" Charity asked, her excitement growing. *This might work after all.*

"My name's Levi, miss," he answered, his face grim. What she said next came as a surprise to the boy.

"All right Levi. This will remain a secret between us on one condition."

"A secret between you and me, miss? What's that?" Sweat formed on his upper lip. How do I get myself in these messes, he wondered.

"I want some buckskin clothes, my size, and in the morning, I want you to introduce me as your cousin to Mr. Mason. I'll pay you for that and for the clothes, but you can't tell anyone else about this. Is that a deal?"

"How much are you willing to pay me?" His already wide eyes widened even more at the thought of having actual money of his own.

"I'll give you two shillings. One now, and the other when you deliver on your part of the deal. You have to promise not to tell anyone about our arrangement, since this is very important to me.

"Two shillings?" His mind reeling, he thought I've never had that much money in my life! "Don't worry miss, I won't tell anyone here that I have any money, or they will take it from me. I'll bring you the clothes early so you'll be ready before dawn, but you'll have to pay for them."

"I'll pay for the clothes and your second shilling after you introduce me as your cousin. If Mr. Mason sees through my disguise, the deal is off. So, outfit me to make a long journey, as if I really am a young man instead of a twenty-year-old woman. It's a good thing I'm taller than most women or this might not work."

Accepting his shilling from Charity, Levi looked toward the hills and back to Charity. She suspected it was longing she saw in his eyes.

"When my indenture is up, I intend to head for those hills. I want to see what's behind that mountain, that one, and the one way over there. I ain't ever coming back to be a servant to anyone."

Charity watched the boy run off on her errand; she smiled, satisfied with the deal she made. Suddenly very tired she made her way to the inn. Built of stout logs and rustic with few amenities, the inn was run by a respectable family, and suitable for ladies traveling alone. She wondered how respectable the family would think her if they knew what she planned to do. Cornhusks in the mattress rustled as she climbed into bed in the tiny room, thinking how different it was from her home.

Dreading the thought that Levi might renege on their deal, Charity barely slept. She had been awake, dressed, and on pins and needles for hours, waiting to see if he'd keep his part of the bargain. It was still dark outside when she heard a soft knock on her door.

"Here they are, miss, Levi whispered, knowing the outrage it would cause if he were discovered inside a lady's room. "I even found some moccasins for you. You won't look much like a boy if you wear them shoes you got on."

"Thank you Levi," she said. From now on, don't call me miss. Call me…, ah, Charles, yes, now I'm Charles. And thanks for the moccasins, I didn't think about my shoes giving me away. Remember now, I'm your cousin. Tell John Mason that I'm thin, but I'm strong, and I don't talk much. Do you have it all straight?"

"Yes, mi…Charles."

"Now turn your back. I know it's pitch black in here, but I'd feel better knowing your back is turned.

"Yes mi…Charles." Still scared by the prospect of being found in Charity's room, he turned and pushed against the stout, split-plank door to keep it closed while she dressed.

Quickly, Charity dropped the long petticoats and long heavy dress she wore, pulling on the unfamiliar leather clothing. The soft buckskin pants and shirt clung to her body as she slid them over her bare skin. She felt almost naked without all the petticoats and long skirts she was accustomed to wearing. Twisting her long blonde hair into a lengthy rope, she tucked it up under the hat and jammed it down low on her forehead.

"All right, Levi," she whispered, "I'm packed and ready. I'll leave my valise downstairs with a note on the table that I met my friends, and I'm checking out early. I will send for my clothes when I find Robert. Now, let's see if we can convince Mr. High and Mighty John Mason that I'm a strong healthy boy, and just the person he needs as his helper."

Slipping into the inky darkness of the stairwell, Charity hoped the stairs wouldn't creak and give them away. She and Levi felt their way to the front door, lifted the latch, and slipped into the night.

They found John busy with his skin-wrapped packets of metal arrowheads, knives, tomahawk heads, ribbons, cloth, and beads. He was mumbling to himself. "The more I carry now, the more wealth I can bring back in prime pelts. I should've asked Levi to find more than one helper."

"God, I wish my head didn't hurt so much," he said, checking his rifle and powder. "That old coot's white lightning is powerful enough to kick like a mule, and I think the mule is inside my head, still kicking." He stopped to rest, hoping the pounding would stop. "Not only do I have a horrible hangover, but my tongue is burned raw. That stuff would eat your guts out. When are them two boys getting here?"

Griping about Levi and his cousin being late, he looked up to find them standing beside him. He jumped up in surprise, which increased the pounding in his aching head. "Holy Damn, if we were in Indian country, you'd have scalped me before I knew it. Damn this hangover."

"This is my cousin…, Charles, Mr. Mason. He's kinda wiry and skinny, but he's strong. He don't talk much so he won't talk your ear off."

John Mason peered at the new boy in the predawn light, doubtful of his thin, wiry frame. Knowing that beggars can't be choosers, however, he needed the help too much to be picky and kept quiet.

Struggling under the weight of his over-stuffed pack, he said, "Damn. They weigh too much. This will wear us out the first day. Damn. Damn, I got greedy and bought too much. Damn. Come on boy, shoulder this pack and let's get on the trail." Charity's knees nearly buckled when he put the heavy load on her shoulders, but she managed to stay on her feet.

Levi, standing nearby, watched them with envy, knowing they were going in the direction he wanted to go, and they needed more help. He knew few would miss him, especially not the stable owner who wouldn't leave his still that long. Stepping next to his newfound cousin, he made the most momentous decision of his young life.

"Mr. Mason, my employer said I could go with you as long as he gets a fair price for my services and a share of the profits when you return. I know where there's another pack we can use. If I carry one, would you let me go with you?"

"You're hired, boy. Go get that pack, and make it quick, we have a long way to go." Relieved beyond words, the trader took his and Charity's packs and got to work redistributing the goods into three stacks.

"If you'll pay me now for finding Charles for you," said Levi, "I could leave it with my employer. It would ease his mind some about me leaving." Mason agreed, and adding the pay from John Mason to the pay given earlier by Charity, Levi ran back to the stable. On his return, he brought a leather carry pack and set to work, helping load the bundles for their trek.

When they were ready, the trader looked at his young helpers and said, "You two will be weak at first. The second day you're going to be so sore you'll think you can't walk. By the third day, we should be making good time. Come on boys, step lively.

Chapter 2

Unused to carrying heavy loads over rough, uneven ground, Charity and Levi struggled to keep up with John Mason's long, easy strides. They dropped exhausted to the ground when he called a rest, gasping for air.

"Come on boys, toughen up," he said, thinking how much easier it was to slip through Indian country alone, since he made little noise and could hide easily at any hint of danger. "If you're going to survive out here, you have to be tough, careful, and quiet. Your heavy breathing can alert any Indians in the area that we're here. It's all right today, 'cause we're in friendly territory, but later we can't make this much noise. Now, with three people and all heavily laden, it will be tougher, and we'll all have to be more vigilant."

Charity stared hard at the trader, thinking him the toughest, meanest man she had ever met. While she and Levi sucked in ragged breaths, he was barely breathing hard; they were covered in sweat while he seemed impervious to the heat.

Looking down at her leather shirt, she was shocked to see her pack's horizontal straps were pulling her breasts up, accentuating them. Quickly, she leaned over, turned her back on the two males and rearranged the broad straps to better hide them.

Fortunately, John Mason was busy searching in his food pack and didn't notice. He pulled out sticks of jerked meat and handed them around.

"Here, this will get you by until we stop tonight. Drink lots of water, we can't afford to have either of you drop behind."

Hungry, Charity clamped the stiff jerky between her teeth and lifted her pack again without complaint. Her stomach was growling from having no breakfast and now, no noon meal. Her shoulders were chafing, and she knew she'd have blisters by nightfall. That's when the humor of the situation hit her, imagining the surprise their slave-driving leader would have if he saw what was under her shirt besides blisters. She grinned to herself, adjusted her pack straps, and followed him.

It was nearly sundown before John called a halt by a small pond. The boys, grateful to drop the heavy loads, sank to their knees in relief, but John Mason barely gave them time to breathe.

"You two can switch tasks each day, but to start out, Levi, you get the firewood while Charles gets the food ready. I'm going to take advantage of the pond and get cleaned up. One of those ladies back there told me I stank, and that won't do in Indian country. Remember this; Indians can smell a white man unless he keeps himself real clean. I don't want to attract anyone that might not be friendly."

Levi and Charles looked at each other, rolled their eyes, and went to work. "I'm glad you came with us, Levi," she said as they built the fire. "I don't think I could have pulled this off by myself."

The food was cooking by the time John strolled back into camp, stark naked, water dripping off his muscled body. His entrance caught Charity off-guard, and she turned her head quickly, trying to hide her blush. She had never seen a young, naked man's body before, and it was burned into her memory forever that day.

"You boys bathe while I finish cooking. It feels good to have the sweat washed off and let the wind dry my skin."

At the pond, Charity and Levi stared at the inviting water, trying to decide what to do. After a long day of sweating, blistering, and aching muscles, the idea of a bath was the single most luxurious end to a day Charity could ask for, but how could she strip down with the man and boy nearby? Thankfully, Levi answered the question stuck in her mind.

"You go over there where those bushes stick out over the water. You'll be private over there. I'll wash here, where I can't see you. We'll both dress before walking into camp."

Charity was grateful for his quick thinking. She desperately wanted to wash the sweat off her body and let the cool water soothe her blistered shoulders. She bathed and then lay back to enjoy the cool water. It felt like she'd only been there a few minutes when John Mason called them to supper.

"Hey you two, come on and eat. You gonna stay out there all night?"

"Disgusting, irritating man," Charity muttered to herself. With no towel to dry off her skin, she did the best she could with her hands, then wriggled her wet body into the tight leather pants and shirt. Was it only this morning she was in her comfortable dress and petticoats?

"I hope he has the decency to be dressed by now," Charity said to Levi as they walked back. Even as she voiced her concern, she saw the image of his taut, naked body striding into camp, his hair wet, his body glistening with water.

John Mason was still in a state of undress when they got back. She tried hard to keep from looking at him but couldn't keep from sneaking a peek every time she had the chance.

By the fourth day on the trail, both boys gained strength and worked out their soreness. John Mason was pleased with their progress, but he still thought Charles was a little weak. He saw the boy wince as he adjusted his shoulder straps and suspected Charles had blisters under his shirt but was too proud to mention it. *Good lad*, he thought.

Levi was working out well, and John Mason was glad for his company as Charles had little or nothing to say all day. One night, sitting around the campfire, the discussion turned to women.

"You two are young to be going so far from home. Is it because of some girl?" Both boys were surprised when he brought up the subject, and to cover Charity's silence, Levi quickly responded.

"No sir," said Levi, "but I'll admit I'm uncomfortable around girls. They giggle, make me blush, and they make me feel clumsy."

"Well, you're still young, your time will come."

"If you say so, sir," Levi answered. "But before Pa died from the fever, he told me to stay away from girls until I'm older."

"Your pa was just trying to protect you, son, that's what parents do. Right now, girls may make you uncomfortable, but when you're older, you'll find they're marvelous creatures."

"Have you found your girl, sir?"

"Yes, I have, but she doesn't know it yet," said the big man. "She's a Cherokee maiden with long black hair and liquid brown eyes that dance when she laughs."

Charity surprised herself by speaking up in her best *Charles* voice. "I've heard Indian women wear very little clothing, and that they're heathens, and that no decent white man should ever look at them." She silently chastised herself for not being able to keep her mouth shut.

John Mason laughed and said, "Well, they may be heathens, but they sure are nice to look at. She's going to cost me a lot of trade goods, but she's worth it."

Barely keeping the disgust from her voice Charity responded saying, "You're going to buy a wife?"

"Not exactly. Her father demands a dowry just like a lot of whites do. He's an important man and her dowry is steep. It may cost me the contents of one of these packs to make her my wife."

"Oh, I thought you were going to open a trading post with the Cherokee with all this stuff." Levi was obviously fascinated with John's story about bartering for an Indian for a wife, but Charity couldn't understand why he wasn't as disgusted as she was.

John laughed again and said, "I can do that after I get Gray Dove."

"Are you in love with Gray Dove?" Charity asked, curious in spite of herself.

"In love? Bah! There's no such thing. I want her, she's beautiful, graceful, and desirable. She's also a good cook. She'll cook for me and keep my bed warm at night. Besides, why shouldn't I have her if I want her?"

Thinking John Mason was the most callous man she'd ever met, Charity asked, "But doesn't she have a say about who she marries?"

"None, her father will decide for her. I know she prefers another, but it won't make any difference. If I get there with the most valuables, I'll get her.

"That doesn't seem fair to the girl."

"Fair? Who said life is fair? I only care what's fair for me," he said. "You need to keep that in mind, Charles. Forget what others told you. Take what you can get while you can get it. I'll take Gray Dove, and then I'll be the only trader allowed to deal in that village. When I have enough to live in style anywhere I like, I won't need Gray Dove anymore, and the other man can have her if he still wants her. That's what I think is fair."

Charity realized then that if she didn't need John Mason's help to find Robert, she'd gladly kill him herself before he ruined Gray Dove's life. She didn't remember ever meeting a more despicable man.

Later, when she and Levi were ready for sleep on one side of the fire with John on the other, she whispered to Levi, "Don't listen to him about women. He's full of horse hockey. I'll bet when he really does find someone to love, a woman who loves him back, he'll change his opinion."

Chapter 3

Each day they walked deeper into the forbidding darkness of thick forest. Downed trees and overflowing creeks from a recent storm blocked the path, forcing them to climb over or go around the dead falls. Their pace slowed as they fought to push their way through, carrying the heavy packs through dense undergrowth with branches whipping them on all sides. In the swamps, flies and gnats swarmed their sweaty faces, adding to the misery they endured. Irritable and sweaty, tempers flared.

"Hurry up, boys!" John Mason ordered in a hushed voice. "Once we get through this swamp we'll get rid of the biting flies. Keep moving, keep moving. Step lively there, Charles. You're always lagging behind. I don't know why you came on this trip. You're sure not much of a frontiersman. If you don't get a move on, I'm going to put a boot to your butt."

Furious with the man, Charity swung around to face him, fists balled up. She spoke through clenched teeth, "Don't you ever touch me!"

***

John threw his hands up. "Hey! Calm down boy. You scare me with those mighty fists. I'm just anxious to get out of this tangle we're in." Laughing, he walked on ahead, thinking about the boy. There were things about Charles that bothered him. With his effeminate ways and lack of muscle, the boy was obviously unsuited for frontier life, and he belonged in a town.

Later, covertly watching Charles, he questioned himself, thinking since when do I notice how another man walks? Maybe I've been without a woman too long, and I'd better get Gray Dove soon.

***

Her temper hot, Charity fumed all the rest of the day; sleep that night did not calm her down. When she woke up the next morning, she glared at John Mason, thinking of ways to make him miserable the first chance she got. *Just wait until I tell Robert what a despicable man his partner is,* she thought to herself.

Mile after mile they trudged, with heads down, tired, thirsty, and sore. When John began stopping frequently, constantly looking and listening, Charity watched him and listened too, but never heard a thing.

Finally, when they stopped on a ridge to scan the valley below, she whispered, "What are you listening for?"

"Sounds."

"I don't hear any sounds."

"Neither do I, and that's what scares me," he said. "The birds aren't singing, and see that deer down there? It just jumped and ran away. That means something or someone is down there. My gut has been screaming all day, and it's never wrong. You two stay here, I'm going down to see what's waiting for us."

He dropped his pack and slid into the trees, leaving Charity and Levi to wait on the ridge. Watching his progress, they saw a branch jiggle not far from him. Before they could give warning, an Indian burst out from the bushes, tomahawk in hand. Charity shut her eyes in horror, imagining what the weapon would do to his head.

Levi watched as John grabbed the raised tomahawk. He and the Indian rolled and tumbled, disappearing from sight.

Suddenly, Charity's eyes snapped open with the realization that without John Mason to lead them, she and Levi would be helpless on the frontier. Quickly, she shrugged out of her pack and told the boy standing frozen next to her, "Come on Levi, there might be more Indians out there, and they could kill John. We have to help him."

"We don't have any weapons, just our knives."

"We have our brains, don't we?" she whispered. Trying to be silent, knowing they were not, together they slunk down the hill to where they had last seen John Mason.

Nearing the undergrowth where he had disappeared, they heard the sounds of a mighty struggle just beyond. Stepping into the clearing they saw Mason fighting desperately for his life with a powerful Indian on top of him and a tomahawk's blade just inches from his throat.

The fighting was intense, the Indian so bent on finishing John off that he failed to hear the underbrush giving way on their approach. Charity grabbed a stout branch, and without a second thought, swung it full force at the Indian trying to kill John. She struck a vicious blow to his hand, breaking his wrist and knocking the tomahawk into the bushes. Levi followed up with a blow to the head. The man collapsed on top of John Mason and breathed no more. John pushed the body away, gasping for breath and covered with sweat and dirt.

He slowly crawled to his hands and knees and said, "Thanks. He about had me and you two saved my life." When he stood up, his right arm hung limp by his side.

"Mr. Mason, what happened to your arm?" cried Charity.

"He hit me on the muscle, and my arm is numb. I'll be all right." He said, rubbing his swollen bicep. "Here, help me strip the body of any food and weapons. You boys make sure to get everything from him that we can use. We're out in the middle of nowhere, and you never leave anything behind you may need to protect yourself. Remember that." Before they rolled the body into a crevice, John took the Indian's scalp clumsily with his left hand.

"Why did you scalp him? Charity asked, her face green and her stomach churning. A look of disgust clouded her face as she swallowed several times to keep from throwing up.

"He would have done the same thing to me," said John, giving the Indian's bow and quiver to Charity to carry. They helped him get his pack on with his still-numb arm, and they left quickly in case there were other Indians waiting to ambush them. The group walked long into the afternoon before stopping for the night. Charity watched John continue to favor his arm.

After setting up camp, Charity turned to him, seeing he was obviously in pain. "Mr. Mason, let me look at your arm," she said almost forgetting to use her Charles voice.

"It's all right. I just need to rest it for a while," he said. "Under the circumstances you can drop the Mr. Mason, just call me John."

Charity refused to give in and motioned to Levi to help her. She spoke with more authority than she felt, saying, "We need to take off your shirt to look at your arm, Mr. Mason…, John." Both were shocked to see his bicep badly bruised with a huge swollen knot now turning blue. His hand was still numb and he could barely move his fingers. His bicep was hot to the touch.

"We need to cool this down, Levi. Bring me some of that cold spring water and some moss." Levi brought the moss and she pressed it to the bruised arm. When the moss warmed from John's body heat, she poured cold spring water on it. She did this over and over, keeping the moss cold and on the massive bruise.

She felt the warmth from John's body as she knelt close to him. Holding the compress on his arm, she studied his face, seeing laugh lines around his mouth for the first time. *He must laugh a lot,* she thought, *but we've never heard it; I wonder why?* Maybe it's from trying to keep us from getting killed; maybe that keeps him stern and sober.

She wondered idly what it would be like to see him with fewer worry lines and more from laughter, then questioned her own motives. *Since when did I start feeling this way about him?* She quickly reprimanded herself. *You don't like him, remember this, Charity. You don't like this man.* But her hands liked the feel of his skin as she held the wet moss on it.

When it was time to turn in, she tied the moss on his arm. She laid her blanket next to his, and several times during the night, she poured cold water on the drying moss. By morning, the swelling had gone down. Charity flexed his arm and massaged the tense muscles until John could feel his fingers and move them easily.

"Thank you, Charles, my arm feels much better," he told her with the first smile she had ever seen on his face.

Levi cooked breakfast, and when they sat down to eat, John said, "You're getting to be a pretty good cook, Levi. You'll make a good frontiersman yet. Now, I need to teach both of you some of the Cherokee language while we travel.

That way, you will get along better in the village. We'll just learn a few words at a time."

When they finished eating and working on a few Cherokee words, John ran his hand over the stubble on his face. "I need a shave, it's too hot here for whiskers." But when he tried to hold the razor, it fell from his trembling hand.

"Damn it. I can't use my right hand and I've never been able to shave with my left hand. I need one of you to do it for me."

"Not me!" Levi said, backing away. He acted like holding cold steel against John's exposed throat was too much for him.

That left Charity who had shaved Mr. Larkin daily before he died. She rolled her eyes at Levi's reluctance and sent him to fetch hot water. She picked up the razor and wiped it clean, took the hot water from Levi, and bathed John's face to soften his beard. Leaning close to his face, she began to shave him with gentle hands, her touch sure.

"Hey Charles, this feel great. I can tell you've done this before," he said, closing his eyes. "I'm just going to relax and enjoy this," he stated as Charity slid the wickedly sharp razor over his face.

***

Intent on her work, Charity moved in to shave under John's chin and over his lips. She felt her entire body flush from the heat of his male body so close to hers. *Steady, Charity, you can do this,* she told herself, taking a deep breath and moving closer to his lips, an act that nearly proved her undoing.

Never in her life had the desire to kiss someone been so strong until that moment. Reminding herself this was the man she despised, she brought herself under control and finished quickly.

John ran his left hand over his freshly shaved face, and finding no straggly whiskers anywhere said, "Thanks Charles. You do a really good job." He watched Charles.

Charity thought he had a puzzled look.

"You aren't as strong as Levi, but I'm glad you came along. My arm would have been useless for days without your help. You know how to heal wounds and give a good shave. Thank you, and I'm sorry for riding you so hard for lagging behind."

"That's all right," she said. "I know I'm not as strong as Levi, and I'll try harder to keep up."

"No, it's all right. I've been driving us hard to get here. We're deep in Indian country now, and from now on, we need to slow down and be very careful, and we have to stay really close together. Today, we'll rest and give my arm more time to heal before moving on. I'll do the cooking since I can do that without using my arm too much."

Later that day Charity felt an old, familiar ache in her abdomen. It was her monthly menses. She had dreaded it since leaving the settlement, wondering how she would handle it. What can I do, she wondered. I can't ask what Indian women do each month without giving myself away.

Pondering her quandary, she realized Indian women used what was available to them, so what would they use? She sat on the bank of the stream, searching for possible answers. At home, she used old rags, but she had nothing like that here. Her eyes skimmed the plants growing nearby, searching for soft and absorbent material. Cattails growing on the bank were noticed, some so ripe they spilled their soft down into the wind. Their tiny seeds spiraled toward the water and bobbed up and down on the ripples. She picked one, rubbing the down between her thumb and fingers and decided it would work. The next problem was something to hold it in place.

Charity remembered John had packed bright ribbons and a few lengths of cloth in her pack. Waiting until he was busy scouting the area, she removed a length of ribbon and a small square of cloth. From the ribbon she fashioned a belt, rolled some cattail fluff inside the cloth and straddled it, stuffing the ends under the ribbon and wearing it just as Indian men wear their breechcloths.

Before they broke camp, she gathered as many cattails as she could fit into the pack she carried. For the next three days, Charity lived in constant fear that her flow would stain the buckskin pants and betray her identity to John. Checking herself each time they rested, she was able to extract the soiled down, careful to hide it under bushes before replacing it with a new pad. Each evening she picked fresh down, when she could find it, adding it to her dwindling supply.

John's gut warned him something or someone was following them. While he had neither seen nor heard anything to make him fearful, he began checking the back trail often, listening for unusual sounds.

Upon reaching the top of a hill, he found a stump from which to search their back trail. Sitting completely still and looking like a statue, not moving a muscle as he watched, caused Charity and Levi to marvel at him.

Suddenly, John rose from his stump and ran toward the boys. "Hustle yourselves," he said quietly, yet urgently. "My gut was right, we're being followed, but not by Indians, by a big brown bear. He's sniffing the air and our trail, and he's coming right along. We need to get out of here as quickly as possible."

"Do bears usually follow people?" Levi asked, when they stopped to catch their breaths.

"They will attack a single person if they decide to, but not usually three people unless the bear is lame. There's plenty of game around here so I can't imagine why he's trailing us, but we need to throw him off our trail somehow. Bears have a fantastic sense of smell and can smell a dead animal for miles."

"Then why don't we give him one?" Charity came out from behind a boulder she'd been on the other side of. She was discreetly relieving herself and changing her soiled, cattail down.

"What do you mean?"

"Can't we kill something and let the bear go for it, instead of us?"

"I don't like to shoot my rifle when I'm traveling so deep in Indian country because sound carries, and it alerts Indians to my position. This time, I'm willing to gamble to get the bear off our trail, because we can't keep running. We'll wear ourselves out. We're going to have to camp at some point, and if we don't do something, it might attack at night while we sleep."

"That sounds like a good way to wake up dead," Levi joked, trying to offset the seriousness of the situation.

Charity watched behind for signs of the bear in the valley below but saw nothing. Looking forward, however, instead of a bear, she saw Indians climbing up on the trail in front of them.

"John, John!" She cried, keeping her voice low. "Indians are on the trail in front of us, and they're going the same way we are."

"That's just great, we have a hungry bear behind us and Indians in front of us." He looked around for a way to escape. "Let's go down this way. I hear a stream, and if we can walk in it, we might throw the bear off, and it will help us avoid any Indians who may be straggling behind."

Following the sound of rushing water, they found it plunging over a cliff into a pool fifty feet below.

"Come on, let's get down to that pool. If we're lucky, there will be a cave behind the falls and we can hide there. Quickly now, I hear him snuffling behind us."

They scrambled down the side of the waterfall, slipping and sliding as they went. They reached the pool, and John searched for an opening behind the spray. Spying a dark cavern he plunged through the falling water and disappeared.

Just as Charity and Levi moved to join him, they saw the bear climbing down behind them as Indians came up the hill toward the pond. They darted through the water, fighting panic, and the spray, and sliding over slick rocks to enter the cavern.

"John, we're trapped." Levi said, shaking water from his hair and rubbing his eyes dry. "That bear is coming one way and Indians are coming from the other, and we have nowhere to run."

"In that case we'll have to stand and fight. Stay in the back and don't make a sound." Whipped by the wind, the watery curtain thinned just enough for them to see what was happening.

The Indians carried in a deer and one prepared to cook some of the meat while others cut strips to dry by the fire. Meanwhile, the hungry bear was hot on the trail of food. There was meat in sight, and he intended to have it, and he didn't care if it was human meat or deer meat. Reaching the clearing, he rose on his hind legs, now standing at least six feet tall.

The Indians had blood on their hands, there was blood on the ground, the deer carcass right there, and the smells drove the bear into a frenzy. He roared and then charged. Caught off-guard, men scrambled for their weapons. The bear, now crazed by the scent of blood, slapped at them, sending them sprawling from his path. Intent on the deer, he snatched it in his powerful jaws, ignored the men, and dragged it from the campsite. The

Indians, having recovered their weapons, now attacked the bear from all sides.

It took several well-placed arrows to finally bring the bear down. Excited, they jumped on it and slashed its throat. Now, not only would they have venison to take back, but also the best prize of all, a bear. The bear would provide fat and fur, along with energy-giving meat.

Charity watched the whole thing, fascinated, as the Indians pulled the deer carcass back to camp and started cutting up both animals.

"Indians don't let anything go to waste," John whispered. "They find a use for everything." He sighed, found a place to sit, closed his eyes, and added, "Now, at least we don't have a bear following. Let me know when they're gone. I'm going to get some shut-eye."

Charity and Levi settled nearby, keeping watch on the clearing below. Charity was glad her monthly time was ending, and she wondered how she would have kept herself clean in the confines of the small cave with two men in such close quarters.

Chapter 4

Back on the trail the next day, Charity became intrigued by the bow she now carried. When they stopped to rest at the top of a ridge, she tried to string it with no success. Finally John, who had been watching her efforts, offered to show her how to string a bow.

"Here, let me show you how that works," he said. "Stand it on end, slip your left leg inside the bow and the string. With your left hand, bend the bow toward the string, using your hip for leverage, and pull the string toward the bow with your right hand."

The first time Charity tried it, she turned the bow the wrong way, then corrected it. Frustrated, she struggled to bend the stiff bow correctly, until John put his hand over hers to help her steady the bow.

"Now, slip your left leg inside the bow," he said as she followed his directions. "That's the way, now pull the bow over your hip, just like that. Yes."

Charity heard his words, but his body brushing up against hers had her senses on overload, and all she wanted was to lean against him. She took a deep breath and stepped away from him saying, "Thanks for the help, John. I get the idea now. When we camp tonight I'll practice with it for a while."

After the lesson, she could only remember how her body reacted to his nearness when he stood behind her, with both his arms around her. Admitting how much she loved the feel of his arms, she asked herself why she responded that way to him. Then, she reminded herself about how he felt toward women, and that he was callous, insensitive, and despicable.

It was Charity's turn to cook when they made camp that evening. She was grateful for the task, as it allowed her hands to stay busy while her mind evaluated this new, ridiculous feeling of affection she had formed for John Mason, one of the roughest men she had ever encountered.

After supper she worked with the bow until she was finally able to string it by herself. But when she attempted to shoot an arrow, the taut bowstring stung her left forearm.

"Ouch!" She yelped.

John who was watching from a distance asked, "Do you need help?"

"Yes," she said. "Surely no one goes around with skinned wrists from shooting arrows."

"Pull your buckskin sleeve down to protect your arm, or tie a leather strip around your wrist like the Indians do," John said, walking over to her. "Here, let me show you how to aim."

Charity should have known better than to ask for help. John was now standing close with his arms wrapped around her. By the time she released the arrow, hitting the target was the least of her worries.

"Good boy!" he said. "You hit that tree. Was that what you aimed at?"

"Sure," she said, but in truth, Charity had no idea what she aimed at. Probably the mountain, she thought, it was a big enough target.

"Keep practicing, you're a natural with a bow," said John. "It will come in handy out here. The bow is silent and deadly. It's not noisy like my rifle which scares game and alerts Indians that we're near. Maybe we should all switch to bows from now on."

Charity appreciated John's praise, and finding she had a natural ability with a bow and arrow was gratifying. In the wilderness, where life often hung in the balance, a woman needed to know more than cooking and cleaning. She almost laughed out loud then, realizing how she was adapting to this rough life. She could only imagine how shocked her Mother and Father would be if they knew she actually enjoyed dressing like a boy in tight fitting pants and shooting arrows at targets.

Charity practiced until it was too dark to see a target and was up before the others the next morning, working to improve her aim. She shot at targets until her arm ached and her fingers were sore, but she felt a glow of satisfaction at her progress.

I need to learn to shoot at moving targets soon. Not many attackers are going to stand still and let me shoot them, she thought. *I'm not helpless anymore. I may even be able to protect myself and help Levi and John, if we are attacked.*

***

The next evening John tied a slab of bark about the size of a man's head to a branch. The bark became a moving target, swinging and twirling in the breeze from the tree Charity used for practice.

"This will give you an idea of what hunting turkey is like," he told her. "If you can hit that piece of bark consistently, then you'll be able to hunt turkeys as well as defend yourself from attacking Indians. Just remember to lead ahead of the target. Don't aim right at it; anticipate its next move."

Charity studied the target as it swirled, twirled, and jerked in the wind, learning its movements. Then she sighted just where she thought it would be on the next swing and loosed her arrow. Her target jumped erratically, twisting from the impact on its side, so she strung another arrow and shot again. This time, she hit the piece of bark on its downswing and saw it shatter against the tree.

John saw Charles graze the target and turned just in time to see the second arrow rip the bark from where it was dangling and pin it to the tree. His eyes widened.

"My God Charles, that was great, can you do it again?" He found another piece of bark and tied it to the same limb, saying, "Now show me you can do that again, I've never seen a greenhorn learn so quickly."

Levi stood aside, watching with a grin.

Her adrenaline was pumping, and Charity could hardly wait until John tied the next target for her so she could shoot again.

When she also pinned that bark to the tree, John seemed unable to comprehend that his weakest helper was a natural archer. He grinned and reached out to shake the boy's hand.

Charity saw the hand coming toward her and started to step back. *Women don't shake hands,* she thought and then remembered, *I'm supposed to be a boy so I must shake hands like a boy.* She took John's hand and tried to apply enough force to make the handshake seem manly.

John slapped Charles on the shoulder with his other hand and said, "Damn! I don't know if I can top that. It looks like Levi and I better start practicing just to keep up with you. I'm proud of you, son.

Charity floated on a cloud from the praise all the rest of the evening, barely touching the food Levi prepared. Eager to practice, Charity sat still long enough to eat her fill before going back with the bow. That night, she slept with it at her side, her fingers grasping the string. For the first time since beginning the trek to find Robert, he was absent from her dreams; nor did she question why she was sleeping on the ground in the middle of Indian Territory.

The next day they saw a flock of turkeys feeding in the distance, heads bobbing as they pecked. They would look around before pecking again.

"See if you can get us some fresh meat for supper," John whispered to Charles. "I think that young Tom right over there would be just right."

Charity nodded, and then sighted the turkey, noting its timing between feeding and looking up for danger. When its head dropped to feed and then reappeared, her arrow caught it. The big bird flopped on the ground, bleeding out, the other turkeys fleeing into the high grass before flying to safety.

"Good shot, Charles!" said John. "We're going to eat well tonight. Pull that arrow out, and clean it real good—you should always try to get your arrow back when you can. You'll need all of them."

They found a stream and made camp for the evening, and then John showed the boys how to dress a turkey and set it to roast over the coals. Later, between bites of roasted turkey John said, "Charles, I'll never gripe about you again. What you can't carry, you sure make up for by your skill with a bow."

Charity, her belly full and her head filled with John's praise, was so happy she was barely aware of her surroundings. Never having any outstanding talent before, she savored the feeling of accomplishment and personal pride. I may hurt tomorrow from my blisters, but I feel good tonight, she mused, drifting into dreamless sleep.

The days were long and hard as they trudged through the forest, ever aware of danger from Indians, wild animals, and the potential for accidents. Drenching storms raged through the mountains, blowing down trees in their path. In close valleys where the wind barely reached below the treetops, they suffered from stifling heat, but they kept on.

Each day, Charity practiced with her bow, experimenting with practice arrows to avoid breaking or losing the good ones. John tied turkey feathers on the shafts and made crude arrowheads for her to use for practice. Each one was different, and he told her it would make her a better archer as she learned to adapt to each arrow's heft.

Late one afternoon, tired and miserable from trying to find ways to cross a meandering river more than once, and with a storm brewing over the mountains, they decided it was time to make camp.

"Come on," said John, mounting a narrow log to cross over the water. "We don't have time to find a bigger log, the river is rising fast from the storm up on the mountain. If we don't cross tonight, it may be too high to cross in the morning."

Leaving his helpers to cross on their own, he made it to the riverbank where he removed his pack and leaned back on a stump to rest. Meanwhile, Levi and Charles were in deep discussion as they prepared to mount the log, but the rushing water prevented him from hearing them.

"Charity, you've got to do it. We can't wait any longer, the river is rising fast."

"I can't, Levi. It's getting dark, the log is too narrow, and I'm tired and scared. I'll stay on this side tonight and come over when it gets light.

Levi searched for a convincing argument and finally came up with, "How are you going to keep bears and cougars away over here by yourself? What if Indians show up?"

His simple reminder that the woods were not merely full of harmless turkeys, but fearless wild men bearing tomahawks, made facing her fear of the narrow log and the rushing water her only option.

Suddenly energized, Charity stood up, shouldered her pack, slid her bow in her quiver, and attached it to her backpack to keep it secure.

"You go first and I'll follow right behind. Don't go too fast." she told Levi.

Watching from the other side, John was relieved when the two boys started over the log. He would have preferred they cross one at a time, but he was glad to see them crossing in the waning light.

When Levi reached the bank, he jumped to the ground, forgetting his terrified partner was still crossing on the log behind him. His forceful leap dislodged the log, and the rising water below undermined it. Charity saw him leap from the log, felt the change, and then saw a tree churning straight towards her. Loaded down by the pack, she couldn't run, so she jerked it off and slung it to the bank with all her might, feeling the log roll under her.

She tried to run the last few feet, but the tree rammed into the log which rolled out from under her. Arms flailing, she flew through the air, vainly fighting to grab the rolling log, but it twisted like a wild thing, turning in the roiling current. The last thing she saw were the shocked faces of John Mason and Levi as she went under.

***

John ran along the bank, jumping stumps, stumbling over river rocks, trying to outrace the log. When it crashed into the riverbank, he saw a small hand holding onto a limb and watched in horror as it slowly slipped into the cold water and disappeared.

Without another thought, he plunged into the roiling, icy water, trying to find Charles before it was too late. He fought to stay above the surface, searching for any sign of the boy. When he saw a patch of buckskin, he lunged for it and missed. Then he saw long hair floating on the surface and tried to reach it to no avail. Finally he grabbed at what he thought might be a shirtsleeve and held tight.

It was Charles all right, his body tumbling in the rough current with his long hair floating behind. With one hand holding the body, he grabbed at the boy's hair with the other. Gaining solid footing, he pulled Charles from the water, carried him to dry land, and then thumped him on the back to drive the water out of his lungs.

Wondering if he had broken any limbs in his fall from the log, John turned his helper over to probe for damage. He found no breaks, but he did find a firm lump.

When he pressed it to make sure nothing was broken, the boy moaned softly. Finding another lump next to the first one, his patient moaned again when he touched it, but remained unconscious.

Intrigued, the man who still had no reason to think his patient was not a young boy, gently massaged both lumps, searching for injuries. When the boy's lips parted and he moaned again, John's eyes widened in surprise and everything fell into place; those lumps were not wounds.

He pulled the shirt up, and what he saw there made him sit back on his heels in surprise. Pale skin and bare breasts drew a response from his body, and he touched those velvety breasts again, watching for a reaction. What he heard then made his hands snap back to his sides.

"Ohhh," she sighed.

Realizing the girl was still unconscious, he shook himself to gain control of his senses. Again, he raised her up and turned her over his arm, pounding her back until more water came out, and her breathing returned to normal. Desire surging through his body, he held her longer than was necessary, enjoying the feel of her naked breasts against his arm. Finally, when she inhaled deeply, taking in large gulps of air, he sat the girl back down, drawing away from her.

She reminded him of someone he had met before, but he couldn't remember the time or place. Surely, he would have recognized such a beautiful woman even if she were disguised as a boy. Then, he recognized her. This was the woman from Mud Flat, the one trying to find Robert Larkin. Granted, he had been incredibly drunk the day before their journey began, but still, he should have realized the deception.

Anger rose up in his chest and he spoke roughly, "What in bloody hell are you doing here? Who said you could come with me? You could have been killed just now, you crazy woman!" Things started making sense as he raged on in his tirade.

"No wonder you couldn't carry the load as well as Levi. I should have paid more attention. No hint of a beard, fine features, an enticing walk."

He stopped short, mesmerized by her exposed torso. Water dripped off Charity's full breasts, her creamy throat was slender, and he longed to kiss his way down the smooth, white skin.

While he had seen Indian women nearly naked, he had never seen a white woman without clothing. White women were modest. Aware now of her nudity, Charity blushed under his intense gaze.

"Take your hands off me, and don't stare at me like that!" she said, turning away, embarrassed.

When she spoke, John jumped like he had been burned. Quickly, he turned to look the other way as she struggled to pull her sodden shirt down. When she was done, he turned again to see her lips were turning blue.

"We've got to get you warm or you'll go into shock," he said in a harsh tone of voice. "Come on, I'll carry you to the campsite."

"Thank you Mr. Mason. That's the first time you've acted like a gentleman since we met," Charity said, ever the lady. On a practical note she added, "How will I get my buckskin clothes dry? Will they shrink?"

"They've been carefully tanned and smoked over a slow fire," he answered in a matter-of-fact voice. "That makes the leather almost waterproof. If we dry them slowly, they won't shrink. By tomorrow, they should be good to wear. Let's get you to a fire so you can warm up."

Her teeth were chattering when he lifted her into his arms, hoping Levi already had a fire burning. She slid her arm around his neck to get closer to his body heat, her head on his chest. Watching her face more carefully than where he put his feet, he stumbled.

Keep your mind on walking, not on how easily she fits into your arms, John told himself. Gray Dove never made him feel this way. The chill dampness of his wet clothes did little to quench the fire in his body.

Levi looked up in relief when John entered the camp with Charity in his arms, but his stare turned to one of anxiety when he saw she had lost her hat and her hair was hanging loose. Knowing the need for pretense was over, he asked, "Is she all right, John?"

"So, you knew? You two were in on this together?"

"Yes sir, I helped her so she could come with you. It was real important to her."

"Why in God's name did you do that? She could have been killed just now."

"I bribed him to help me," Charity said through chattering teeth. "I needed to go with you, and you wouldn't let me, so this seemed the only way. You are a stubborn man, John Mason, especially when you're drunk." Her teeth chattered uncontrollably, accompanied by severe chills.

John's mind whirled knowing the game had changed considerably with her near drowning; he had to get them through hostile Indian country safely, and now, he had a white woman to protect. Dripping wet, her hair stringing loose around her face, he studied her, savoring every line and curve of her sensual body.

"Let's get this fire burning hotter, Levi," he said, suddenly concerned about her immediate physical need for warmth. "Her lips are already blue and she's freezing. We can't let her die out here."

Although John's anger with Charity was powerful at first, it began to ebb as he came to terms with the situation—that of having a woman along on a long journey. Admittedly, Charity was a clever woman and good at disguises. She had pulled her own weight on the journey without complaint and worked hard, and what she could do with a bow was amazing.

The drawbacks were real enough; if the Indians found out he had a white woman with him, there could be trouble. At the same time, he had to admit he liked the thought of having her with them. He couldn't understand how Robert left her behind, because if she had been his woman, he would never have left her.

John and Levi worked fast to stoke the fire which Levi had built close to a large boulder to capture the heat. They soon had the small fire blazing hot. Then he laid down a ground sheet for her to lie on between the fire and the boulder. Holding up a blanket to give her some privacy as she shed her wet buckskins, John waited until she lay down on the warm ground sheet covered with one blanket, before covering her with two more blankets and the other ground sheets. The heat soon made her drowsy, and she drifted off to sleep with the two men watching over her.

With sunset, the night air grew chilly, and John saw Levi shiver when he lay down to sleep without his ground sheet and blanket. He couldn't risk having Levi get sick, so he took Levi's blanket and ground sheet off of Charity and handed them to the boy.

When Levi realized what he was doing, he protested, "No, she needs those. I can get by."

"Take them, Levi, I don't want you sick. You go on to sleep now. I have to get out of my wet clothes and get warm, too. I'll lie behind her so our combined body heat next to the fire will keep her warm enough.

John checked on Charity who appeared to be sound asleep. He carefully tucked the blankets close, trying not to disturb her, but his touch roused her anyway. With absolutely no shame, she watched through half closed eyes as he removed his soggy buckskins, shivering in the cold, high-mountain air. Goosebumps pimpled his muscular body as he rigged branches to hold their clothes up near the fire. Unaware his patient was watching, he glanced at her often, looking forward to sleeping next to her.

Charity feigned sleep when he lay down beside her. His damp, exposed skin, cold through the blankets, chilled her. Knowing she had a naked man lying next to her and one she had to keep healthy, she turned on her side and casually helped one of the blankets slide over him.

Unaware she was awake, John gently placed one arm over her warm body and snuggled his chin against her neck. Before he knew it, he responded to her and felt instant desire.

Warm in his blanket next to the fire, Levi got up during the night to feed the fire; he smiled when he saw John and Charity nestled together. They were both covered and needed nothing more from him, so he crawled under his blanket and went back to sleep.

John awoke at daybreak to find himself warm, rested, and comfortable. He snuggled closer to the source of the warmth and realized he was completely naked and sleeping next to a desirable woman with his hand on her breast.

Trying not to disturb Charity, he raised the blanket to get up. On the perfect skin of her shoulders, he saw raw and angry blisters that had burst, scabbed over, burst again, and now, had formed open sores. Not once had she complained.

His first impulse was to cuss at her for being so stupid. John realized she couldn't very well have complained, as he would have needed to care for them, and it would have exposed her identity. Now that he knew about those sores, however, they would have to be treated whether she liked it or not.

Leaving the covers on her, John rose to check the buckskins, shivering in the nippy morning air. Their clothes, though still damp, were dry enough to wear.

***

Charity watched everything he did from under the edge of her blankets. He was a muscular man and it gave her great pleasure to watch him dress next to the dancing fire. She blushed when he adjusted his manhood down in the front, but she didn't take her eyes off of him. She particularly appreciated the small patch of hair near the center of his broad chest and wanted to run her fingers through it before he pulled his leather shirt down.

Mortified by her own lascivious thoughts, she raged at herself, saying under her breath, "I don't like that man, I don't like him," even though her face flushed at her thoughts. She couldn't stop thinking about his hand on her breast during the night or the pleasure it gave her. The notion of her breasts as objects of pleasure was new to her. In her mind, they were only for feeding babies, but she had to admit men did seem to enjoy looking at them, even Robert's father when she leaned over his bed.

John woke Levi, nudging him with his foot. "Start making breakfast, I've got to doctor Charles'…, Charity's shoulders.

John dug in his pack, looking for herbs he needed for her sores and spent several minutes grinding and mixing the concoction. Since she was still asleep, he gently lowered the blanket to expose her blistered shoulders.

The minute he moved the blanket, her eyes flew open, and she said indignantly, "What do you think you're doing?"

"Lie still," he told her. "I saw your shoulders, and I'm trying to help you. We have to keep your blisters from getting infected."

"Let me see what's in your hand."

John opened his hand to show a small tin with a mixture of bear grease and herbs he had prepared. "I made a poultice that should help them heal faster. Now be still and let me put it on you."

Satisfied he was trying to help, she turned on her stomach so he could reach both her shoulders. His touch was light and gentle as he applied the greasy mixture over her raw skin, his fingers barely touching her shoulders. When she sighed softly, John jerked his hand away, saying, "Sorry, I didn't mean to hurt you."

"You didn't, it's the first time my shoulders haven't hurt since the blisters formed. Please don't stop."

"That's the second time you've begged me for something," he said, applying the mixture to her skin. "I'm beginning to like it."

"Don't get used to it, it may never happen again," she teased with a grin. "How will I wear my shirt without getting grease all over it? Won't the buckskin absorb it?"

"I found some moss that helps heal also. We'll use it to make a pad to hold the poultice to your shoulders and protect your shirt at the same time. The extra padding will help keep those straps from rubbing against your skin, too."

"Thank you, even though I know you're just helping me so I can carry my pack better. Those places have been painful for days, and sometimes I wanted to scream when they hurt, but I couldn't. I really appreciate what you are doing for me."

Suddenly, she thought about the pack she had thrown to shore before her wild fall. "My pack. Did I lose my pack in the river?"

"No, you threw it to the bank before you fell, and Levi retrieved it. For that, I'll forgive you almost anything, including deceiving me." He said, standing and capping his ointment.

"Are you just going to stand there or are you going to hand me my clothes?"

"It's a nice view I'll have to admit," he said with a wicked grin. I think I'll stand here for a while and think about what's under those covers, and then I might hand you your clothes."

Still lying on her stomach, she pulled the blanket over her head and held out one arm for her clothes. John exhaled noisily in defeat and brought them to her.

Charity managed to pull her pants on under the blanket before asking, "Don't you need to put the moss on my sores before I put my shirt on?" With that said, she turned away and holding the covers under her arms and over her breasts, exposed her pale back to him.

When nothing happened, she looked over her shoulder to see both men staring at her. From the way Levi was looking, his mouth agape, Charity realized this was probably the most female skin he had ever seen. John stood behind her, transfixed at the sight of her unprotected skin.

When a quick feeling of jealousy came over her, it caught her off guard. It irritated her that John had, more than likely, seen his share of bare flesh, and she wondered why it bothered her so much. She was an engaged woman, and John Mason's affairs should mean nothing to her. She was never jealous of Robert, so why was she jealous of John Mason?

"Come on, you two, don't leave me exposed like this," she told them sternly. "John quit gawking and put the pads on my shoulders so I can get dressed and eat. I'm hungry and we need to get going."

John quickly tied the moss over the sores on her shoulders. As a bonus, he got a wonderful view of her breasts when he helped her pull the leather shirt over her head.

Charity noticed he seemed uncomfortable, and he kept shifting positions. He had a strange look in his eyes. She wondered if it was passion. John straightened her shirt without a word and walked away.

The experience made Charity think back to her former life as a protected and treasured daughter living on a plantation. There, she would never have allowed a man to see her ankle, much less her bare back and breasts. If it were known they had slept nude next to each other, no matter that it was for the sake of survival and that John had seen so much of her, it would have created a scandal, one she could never live down. In the wilderness, modesty wasn't all that important to her, but survival was.

Chapter 5

As they continued on their journey, John's attitude changed. He no longer swore at the drop of a hat. He took more breaks and made sure Charity's sores were healing well. He insisted on changing the moss pads daily.

As a result, Charity had to remove her shirt, holding a blanket around herself, while he applied the salve, attached fresh pads, and sneaked brief glimpses of her lovely young breasts as he helped her dress.

Due to the care he took, the sores began to heal, a fact for which Charity was thankful as it made carrying the pack a lot easier. When her load got lighter, she suspected John, or Levi, or both, had taken some of the weight from her pack and absorbed it into theirs.

The next couple of weeks on the trail proved to be uneventful. With her shoulder sores healed, Charity began practicing with her bow and taught Levi how to shoot it, too. Soon Levi and Charity were competing for best shot. While it was obvious Levi could shoot farther with his stronger arm muscles, Charity still out shot him.

John fashioned a bow for Charity to fit her size and strength and gave the captured one to Levi. Then he made a stronger one for himself.

"My rifle is deadly, but it's loud and makes smoke. If we use bows, we can kill silently and not alert Indians or scare game away."

John watched them practice and when Charity's shirt pull tight as she aimed at the target, she noticed. He was looking at her neck and lips. John still believed she was Robert's wife so all he did was watch."

***

Levi knew John and Charity were avoiding one another, and not doing a very good job of it. Later, sitting around the fire, Levi sat concentrating on his fingers, a frown on his face. He looked up to see his companions watching and held up his hands.

"If I've figured it right, today is my birthday," he told them. "I just turned eighteen, so I'm no longer a boy."

"Happy Birthday, Levi," said John. But are you sure it's today?"

"I figured it this way, before we left the settlement my birthday was seven weeks away. We've been gone about that long, and I have it figured pretty close, so it's one day this week. Today is as good a day as any."

"Happy Birthday, Levi," Charity said, giving him a light kiss on the cheek as John watched. Levi suspected John was thinking how much he'd like to have her lips on his cheek.

***

Rummaging in one of the packs John pulled out a hunting knife in a scabbard and gave it to Levi. "Here, Happy Birthday. What brought you to Mud Flat? Why were you an indentured servant?"

"My Pa owned a livery stable back east," Levi said, looking down at the ground, remembering. "I was their only living child, as he and Mama lost the others, either at childbirth or as infants, from fever or the pox. I remember how heartbroken Mama was each time a young'un died. She would be melancholy for weeks afterwards." Still looking down, he took a twig and scratched a circle in the dirt.

"I was just a young boy then, but it worried me to see her so sad. When the pox came around again, Mama was still weak from having her last baby, and she came down with it. She had no strength to fight, but she hung on for two weeks before giving up. My pa liked to have gone crazy. He started drinking after Mama died, and he stayed drunk for weeks at a time. I tried to run the livery stable by myself, but people knew what was going on, and they cheated me. I was just a kid. Who could I turn to?" He drew another circle inside the first one and continued with his story.

"Pa ran up a lot of feed bills, and people were renting horses and buggies without paying, and the bills got bigger. Pa couldn't pay them; so to cancel the debt he indentured him and me for five years each. I was only eleven at the time we were indentured, but Pa didn't live out his five years. So, they added his remaining year to mine, and I still had that extra year to go when we left Mud Flat. Now, I'll never go back. I'll live alone in the mountains, or I'll live with the Indians before I'll be a slave to any other man."

Charity asked John, "What about you, John? Where did you come from?"

***

Instead of answering the question, John raised his arms, stretched and yawned, saying, "We better hit the hay. We have a long trek tomorrow and most of it's uphill." It was as if he didn't hear her question.

With a groan, Charity turned to her bedroll and prepared to sleep. She was drifting off when she realized John had avoided talking about his former life. Why, she asked herself? What wouldn't he want us to know? She answered her own question before her eyes closed, thinking he was probably just as tired as she was.

Each day they traveled deeper into hostile Indian Territory. John knew they'd been lucky to have only two serious encounters up until then. They trudged along silently, careful to leave as little sign as possible. Every day John prayed no hunting parties found their tracks. He knew skilled hunters could tell by the footprints that they were white, and by now, that Charity was a woman, making them more likely to attack. Heavy footprints meant a heavy load and plunder and were an open invitation for an ambush.

When John's intuition stirred, and he began constantly checking their back trail, both Charity and Levi acted nervous. Their worst fears were confirmed when he left them to backtrack and came running back, saying, "We are being followed by a war party, seven of them. They look young, so I think this may be their first time at war, but that's still too many for me to fight alone. We have to come up with a plan."

John knew if they were caught, he and Levi might roast over a slow fire or be forced to carry the packs to the village and then be roasted in front of the whole tribe.

From John's experience, he realized Charity was the greatest prize. He also knew he would kill Charity himself before he'd let the Indians take her off to their camp. But what if he were killed first, what then?

He turned to Levi with a somber expression. "Levi, if I'm killed, I want you to promise me you'll not let them take Charity alive. Kill her!"

Shocked, Charity gasped, her face turning white with fear.

Levi's mouth suddenly went dry, and he stuttered, "I c…, can't do that. Why would I kill her?"

"You have to, boy," John said, his expression stern. "If you don't, after they torture you, they'll take her as a prize. Do I have to explain what it might mean for her?"

Levi, still pale, looked first at John and then at Charity. If she were captured she might be taken as a wife, adopted as a daughter, or she could be tortured and used as a sex slave by the men of the village. None of the options appealed to him.

He swallowed hard, looking at Charity, and said to John, "I will kill her, before they kill me."

***

Charity, realizing the seriousness of their situation, listened to the whispered conversation and saw their stricken looks as they talked about killing her. Finally, she could stand it no longer and said, "Now, wait just a minute. Don't I have any say in this plan for my execution?"

Both men looked at her and said in unison, "No!"

"Well, if our situation is so bad, why don't we do something about it?"

"What do you mean?" At this point, John was willing to grasp at straws.

"You said there are seven of them," she said. "There are three of us, so why don't we reduce the odds?"

"Yeah. Let's ambush them." Levi said, pulling out his bow.

"Why not?" Charity added. "They wouldn't expect us to attack them, after all we're traders and laden down with goods, and they won't expect us to be fighters. Am I right or not?"

John looked from one to the other, "She has a point. How confident are you two with your bows? Do you think you could shoot a man instead of a defenseless chunk of bark or a Tom turkey?"

"Since our lives depend on it, yes," Charity said, already stringing her bow. She looked at Levi, his lips were tight, his eyes determined as he strung his bow.

John found a small clearing around a fallen hickory tree. The stump had rotted and around it a circle of tiny saplings had taken root, providing no shield. Indians caught in the clearing would be clear targets for the archers.

"When I say so, throw your packs down and run out of this circle. Levi, you run behind the blackberry bushes. Charity, you hide behind those bushes, and I'll be between you two. That way, we'll have a clear field of vision and can catch them in the crossfire. If you can, hit them low, a gut shot is best. It doesn't kill them right away, and they have to carry off the wounded. Are you sure you can do this?"

Both looked a bit green and their hands were shaking, but they nodded in agreement.

"Won't we leave tracks when we run for the bushes?" Levi whispered. "Won't they know where we went?"

"I'm counting on them knowing we ran. If I'm right, they'll think we got scared and ran off, leaving them free to plunder. Ready? Go!"

***

Crouched and waiting in the bushes, Charity's heart beat hard, her mouth was dry and her hands wet with sweat. She saw a twig move on a tree and thought her eyes were playing tricks on her. When it moved again and a painted face peeked through the leaves, she held her breath and waited.

A young warrior slipped into the clearing, his eyes alert, looking at the packs and over at the running footprints. Grinning, he motioned his six men to join him in the clearing. Young and inexperienced, greed overcame caution, and they ran to the packs. Laying their bows aside and caution to the wind, they quickly began to untie the flaps.

John loosed his first arrow, hitting a man low in the kidneys. At the same time, an arrow struck one man in the neck, and another was hit in the femoral artery. The four warriors remaining grabbed their bows and crouched, trying to see where the arrows came from. John took a long stick and shook a branch, attracting attention.

All four shot toward the shaking limb, missing John, while Charity and Levi took down two more of the warriors. The remaining two tried to slink away, but John and his archers took them down.

When John, Charity, and Levi walked into the clearing, only one Indian raider was still alive, jerking slightly before he lay still.

"Are you two all right?" John asked, looking them over for injuries.

"Ye…, yes," Charity said as shock from what she had just seen and done descended on her. "I was afraid you were hit when they all shot at the branch you shook."

"I was lying on the ground, I shook the branch and rolled away fast. Otherwise, I'd look like a pincushion," he said, grinning.

Levi stared at the dead men. "I didn't think I could do it. I just killed men."

"You just killed some men that would have slit your throat without a second thought. They would have lifted your hair and eaten your food while sitting next to your body. Remember that when you start feeling guilty about it."

Levi nodded, turned and ran into the bushes where they heard him retching.

"How about you, Charity? It's all right if you need to vomit. Lots of people do the first time they kill."

"All I have to do is think about what they would have done to me had we not killed them first, so no, I don't need to throw up, I'm fine."

"I couldn't have survived without you and Levi. Thank God you learned to use that bow and then taught him. There was no way I could have stood them off by myself."

"You're being kind. Without us, you would have left fewer tracks, and I think you would have been all right," she said, smiling up at him.

They took the Indian's weapons and food before rolling the bodies down into a gully. "I should scalp them so it will look like other Indians killed them," said John. "But you and Levi still look a little queasy, so I won't do it this time. Scalps are valuable to Indians. They believe they can't go to their heaven without their hair, so I guess we'll let these young men go to heaven."

Knowing when the bodies were found the Indians would come after them with a vengeance, they put miles behind them as fast as they could before making camp for the night.

They ate a light meal but neither Charity nor Levi had much appetite. Levi turned in early but did not sleep. As he moved towards his bedroll he said, "It never occurred to me I might have to kill another human being to survive, much less right after my eighteenth birthday. I guess to live on the frontier, I need to toughen up.

***

John and Charity sat at the fire, both deep in their own thoughts. For the first time since meeting John at the settlement, she felt free to ask about Robert.

"How much farther before we find Robert?"

"We have two more weeks of rough, hard travel before we get close," he told her. "The trail just gets rougher the farther we go. Do you think you can take it?"

"I don't have much choice, as I surely can't go back now. I'll just get tougher like you told Levi and 'Charles' back when we started."

"I'm sorry I was so rough on you back then. If I'd known you were a woman—"

"If you'd known I was a woman you wouldn't have let me come on this dangerous journey with you. I understand it—you thought we were both boys. Can I ask you a personal question?"

"Maybe." He watched her for a moment, then said, "Yeah, I guess so."

"What you said that first night about not believing in love. Did you mean that?"

"At the time I did," he said gently, avoiding her eyes.

"Are you still going to take Gray Dove as your wife even though she loves another?"

"Why do you care about her? She's just a heathen, you said so yourself." He was deep in his own thoughts, and he did what no one on the frontier should ever do. He stared directly into the fire. As a result, his eyes would take critical seconds to adjust if he was attacked.

"Heathen or not, she's still a woman," Charity said. "She needs to feel loved."

"Did Robert make you feel loved?" he asked, finally turning toward her.

"That's none of your business." She rose to leave.

"Oh, I see, it's all right for you to ask me personal questions, but I can't ask any of you. Is that fair?"

Charity hesitated and sat back down with a sigh. "What do you want to know?"

"Why Robert never told me he was married? He and I have been partners for almost two years now, and we've talked about many things. I know how he felt when his mother died and I know he came from money. I know he's well educated, but never once did he ever mention being married. Especially to a woman as pretty as you, now, why not?"

Charity turned red, dropped her head, then looking toward her blanket she started to get up.

John grabbed her hand and turned her around to face him. "No you don't. You aren't ducking out on me. Answer my questions. Why didn't Robert tell me he was married? Men don't go into the wilderness leaving beautiful, desirable women behind without mentioning them at least once."

"I can't tell you," she said, her voice barely audible.

"Why can't you tell me? What could be so shameful that you can't speak of it? Did you cheat on him?"

Hurt showed in her eyes, she thought about slapping him. Biting her lip to keep back tears, she took a deep breath and said, "No. I didn't cheat on him. I never had the chance to cheat on him, because he left me practically at the altar! Now, are you satisfied?"

Those words made John a very happy man. She wasn't married. He continued to hold her hand, stroking her fingers, encouraging her to continue with her story.

"The wedding, only three months away, was all planned. Instead of facing me to tell me he didn't love me, he just slunk off without a word, and I need to know why. He doesn't even know his dad died last year, leaving him considerable property. I promised Mr. Larkin before he died that I would find Robert, and that's what I'm doing here.

"When Robert disappeared it really hurt his dad, and Mr. Larkin slowly lost interest in living. When he finally took to his bed, I took care of him since he was the closest thing to family I had. I was shocked when he told me he changed his will, making me executor, until Robert returns to take over. But if he doesn't return in two years, the property becomes mine. I don't want his land. I must tell him so he can assume his rightful inheritance."

"Tell me this," John said, drawing her into his arms, "Did Robert make you sigh when he did this?" He softly touched his lips to hers.

Ohh, oh no," she said. "He never did that."

"No? Did he ever kiss your beautiful lips like this?" He held her head in his hands, smothering her mouth with his own, taking his time, until she slid her arms around his neck and met his kiss fully.

"Or did he ever touch you like this?" His fingers gently massaged her breasts beneath her leather shirt. John knew what he was doing and decided any man who could leave this woman behind did not deserve her. Passion surged through him, and he walked away from her, going into the woods alone.

Flushed and breathing hard, Charity lay down on her blankets and began to replay the memory of John's lips on hers and his hands on her breast.

Robert's light and passionless kisses never made her feel the way John's had done just now. While she might have welcomed more from her fiancé, his fingers never touched anything but her hand.

Charity stayed awake, thinking, long after John returned from the woods and turned in. Now that she understood what the word passion meant, she had to admit Robert had never aroused such feelings in her.

The new conflict in her head was more confusing than the battle she had waged in deciding to make this journey. She had begun the trek on a quest to find Robert and bring him back, hopefully as her lawfully wedded husband. But, much had changed in their time on the trail.

She had never known real passion before meeting John Mason. While they were attracted to each other, was it really love, and was it enough for her? In spite of her skills with a bow, she was a refined woman who longed for marriage and a family. She had already wasted a lot of time fighting Indians and climbing mountains, looking for Robert, but did she want to traverse the frontier for the rest of her life?"

When she finally slept, it was to dream of Robert and John. They were standing on a hill with an Indian woman standing between them. She ran toward Robert, but seeing her coming, he turned away to look at the Indian woman. John, however, welcomed her with open arms.

The fire had burned low when Charity woke from her dream. Wide-awake, she fed sticks into the coals and stirred up the fire, wrapped a blanket around herself and sat staring at the flames, thinking about the dream. Why had Robert turned to the Indian woman without speaking to her? What about the feelings John had aroused in her? What did it all mean?

John appeared to sleep soundly nearby, and she watched him, thinking back on the dream. While she was tempted to kiss the sleeping man, instead she touched his lips with her fingers and crawled back to her bed. John's eyes flickered open when she left him.

Sleep was slow in coming to Charity, however. Thoughts of Robert, Gray Dove, and John played through her mind. What was she doing with John out here in this wilderness? Why did she dream about him, long for him, and ache for his caresses when his heart was set on winning Gray Dove back, and she belonged to Robert?

Finally, in plain terms, she asked herself why she wanted John Mason. She admitted it was because she loved him. She realized her feelings for Robert were those of a sister for a brother, not a lover. What she felt for John was deep longing. She was in love.

The next morning, her heart light, Charity got up before the men and built the fire to broil meat and cook cornmeal mush.

***

John awoke and vaguely remembered Charity leaning over him during the night. She had touched his lips lightly. He did not know why, but the thought made him smile. He saw Charity bending over the fire. He fought the sudden wild impulse to grab her and pull her against him, but then reminded himself that she was probably anxious to get to Robert.

So be it, he thought, no matter what happens, the quicker we eat, the quicker we can get on the trail, and the sooner she can be with Robert.

At some point, he knew it would be necessary to tell Charity about Robert and Gray Dove, and he dreaded it. How could he tell her about the day he found Robert holding Gray Dove, kissing her with a passion she obviously welcomed? The betrayal and anger he felt towards his friend had consumed him for some time, and was so strong that he declared he'd win Gray Dove. Now he knew the vow was meant as a challenge to Robert more than love for the woman. As he thought about it, he realized Gray Dove had faded to a distant memory—he no longer wanted her.

John, shocked by his own emotions and thinking about the situation he was in, wondered if Robert felt an ounce of the turmoil he experienced over Charity. He felt he had betrayed Robert with Charity. John was in a black mood as they traveled, brooding most of the day. He snapped and barked at the other two, and when they stopped to rest, he stood away from them, leaning against a tree, saying no more than he had to.

Without knowing the cause of his anger, Charity and Levi kept out of his way, saying as little as possible and trying not to cause him displeasure. That night they practiced archery and turned in early, all without saying a word to John Mason.

The next morning, Levi made a good breakfast, hoping John would snap out of his foul mood. It didn't work, and soon, Levi and Charity were feeling the effects of his temper.

So deep was he in his melancholy that a brush with danger failed to shake him from it. Seeing leaves shaking on the trail below, he motioned quickly and said, "Indians down slope. Get back and load your bows."

As one, they slid into the shadows and watched the men make their way through the undergrowth. When they passed on, John made them stay still until he was sure the party was gone.

"I think we're safe now," he told them. "While I don't think they were looking for us, it doesn't make the situation any less dangerous. If they shift their path to the right, they'll run into our tracks and you can be sure, if they do, they will change course and follow us."

John heard himself speaking in the same biting tone he had used all morning and hoped his tone wouldn't make things any worse. Protecting Charity was all that mattered to him, and to do it, they had to know the danger they were in and be as vigilant as he was.

"I'm surprised we haven't had a run in with more warriors since we killed the ones in the clearing. It makes me more wary than ever," he said.

"Well then, there's no sense in wasting time, is there, Mr. Mason?" said Charity with a bite in her own voice. "Let's get moving and hope they don't find our tracks. I'd like to put as much distance between us and them as possible. After all, I'm not keen on having either of you kill me or on becoming the tribe's prize white woman." With that declaration, she stalked away from them, leaving the other two to follow in her wake.

That night, after they set up camp, John stood to the side, staring into the distance. Finally, he gathered the canteens and took them down to the stream. After he filled them, he sat back on his haunches to think about life without Charity. He knew he couldn't stay to watch her go to Robert. He was also concerned about Gray Dove. Would she get a broken heart, too?

Levi and Charity watched him go and took matters into their own hands. Levi stayed in the camp to clean up, and Charity made her way down to the stream where John was sitting.

He heard her coming, stood up, and turned to face her with every intention of making her go straight back to camp, but she didn't give him the opportunity.

She stood with her hands on her hips and faced him. With a glare, she pointed her finger at him and started in. "I don't know what your problem is John Mason, but you can take it out on something besides Levi and me. We are tired of your bad humor. If it's about me, that's one thing, but leave Levi out of it, because I won't have him treated this way. You have no right to act this way towards us."

In her anger, she stood so close to him he found himself backing up, closer and closer to the streambed until he lost his balance. He threw his arms out to stay steady, and Charity caught him by the arm, allowing him to regain his footing.

Unaware of what she was doing, she held on even after his feet were planted securely on the bank. Without thinking, John put his arms around her and kissed her deep and long, gazing into her eyes.

"You sure know how to tell a man off," he said without breaking eye contact, his mouth close to hers. "But I like the way it ends. Let's do it some more."

Assuming her consent, he kissed her until she was out of breath before pulling away. When he smiled at her, her heart did a double thump, and her mouth went dry at the look in his eyes.

"You know I'm in love with my best friend's fiancé, don't you?" John asked, holding her head gently against his chest.

"If you mean me, as far as I'm concerned, Robert broke our engagement when he left." Her voice was soft when she spoke, muffled next to his heart. "He's found someone else, hasn't he? Gray Dove, right?"

"How did you know?"

"Woman's intuition. You planned to take her from him. Do you still want her?"

"No, that was only out of spite," he told her. "It was a senseless attempt to even the score after Robert took our partnership for granted. I've never felt this way about a woman before, and I'm beginning to understand how, sometimes, people forget the rules when they fall in love." He kissed her once more.

"I want you with me. I want to wake each morning with you in my arms and I want us to grow old together. Until I met you, I never thought about such things, but now, you're all I think about.

He pulled back, and watching her face very carefully, asked, "Do you care for me, even a little?"

"Not just a little, John Mason, I care for you more than life itself. I love you. I only thought I loved Robert, but now I know he's like a brother to me. You are my love. What do we do now?"

"Right now, I just want to hold you and know that you love me. That's the greatest gift you can ever give me." They stood on the stream bank for some time, holding one another, completely oblivious to the potential for danger.

***

Back at the camp, Levi was concerned about them, fearing they might have stumbled into a nest of Indians. When he found them wrapped in each other's arms, he crept back into camp with a smile on his face. "It's about time they found out they love each other. Maybe John won't be so irritable from now on."

When John and Charity returned to camp bringing the filled canteens with them, Levi saw the happiness on their faces. At first, he said nothing, watching the small attentions that betrayed them. Finally, when he could stand it no longer, he burst out with, "Why don't you two just admit you're in love? I can see it all over you. You can't hide it."

"How did you know?" they asked him.

"I've known it longer than either of you have, and it sure has been a learning experience! My pa may have left me with some advice about women, but this has been a lesson on its own. I knew you would get there, eventually, but I was really hoping you would realize you were meant for each other before we got to the village. I'm happy for you both." He gave Charity a hug, shook John's hand, and said, "If this doesn't brighten up our days on the trail, I don't know what will. Some journey this has been, and that's for sure."

Chapter 6

While he was still wary, watching for Indian sign, John's mood had lightened considerably. It was obvious he enjoyed the way the fringe on Charity's shirt slid over her hips as she walked nearby, and as Levi had hoped, the next few days on the trail were pleasant.

When they found signs of activity on the trail belonging to different groups, John determined there was a war going on up ahead. From the tracks they saw, all the war parties were headed in the same direction as they were.

"We're going to have to detour around these war parties, even though this is the most direct trail," he told them. "The safest way is to take the path around and then over that mountain yonder. It will add miles to our journey, but it's seldom traveled and safer."

Charity thought the beaten path they had trod was hard to traverse, but the route they took for that portion of the journey was like nothing she had ever seen, with downed trees, brambles to slap their faces, and rocks strewn over what little path there was.

Hot, tired, and thirsty, both Charity and Levi were on the verge of collapse when John decided to set up camp next to a small spring.

After she finished her chores, Charity found a small pool near the spring and knelt down to wash her face. Hearing an unfamiliar voice in the silence, her head snapped up at the sound, but she stayed where she was, close to the ground and next to the water.

"Halloo, the camp," called the stranger's voice.

"If you're friendly come ahead," John replied, holding his rifle ready.

Hidden by dense undergrowth, Charity saw a white man carrying a rifle walk into camp. Something about him made the hair on the back of her neck stand up.

"I am Samson Wallace. I've been following your tracks for miles, and I know there are three of you, so tell the other one to come on out. I'm friendly." Watching for the third member of their party, Wallace continued, "And in whose camp am I now a guest?"

My name is John Mason, and that's Levi Collins. Charles is getting wood for the fire. Sit down for a spell." It was customary on the frontier to offer food and drink to the wayfarer, but John's instincts told him Samson Wallace was trouble and forbad the courtesy to him.

"I saw from your tracks you're packing heavy loads," he said, his eyes sweeping the camp. "Are you a trader?" From the expression on his face, he seemed pleased with what he had seen thus far.

"I trade with the Cherokee, they're expecting me soon," John responded.

"Ah yes, the Cherokee—they are a fierce tribe," said Samson Wallace. "I don't know how you made friends with them; I never could."

"I take it you're not traveling alone so you must have friends, Indians maybe," said John.

"Yes, I have friends," said Wallace with a ghost of a smile that was more of a smirk. "Nobody travels alone out here."

"What tribe?"

"Oh, different ones. It seems we gain a few here and there. You know, the ones who leave their villages for greener pastures."

"There seems to be a lot of Indians on the warpath right now, John said. "Have you noticed?"

"Oh yes, they are all stirred up," Wallace replied without offering more information than was needed.

"Do you know why?" John persisted, refusing to back down.

"I hear the French are arming Indian tribes again to attack the British on the frontier. This will be a very dangerous place from now on."

"I'm sure it will be dangerous," John agreed. "I've heard there are renegade whites and Indians roaming around attacking both Indian villages and English towns. Have you heard about that?"

"Yes, yes I've heard that too," Wallace said, looking around again. "It's just shocking what some people will stoop to these days. Say, isn't that boy taking a long time to find firewood? There's plenty laying around."

"Well, maybe Charles is taking a dip downstream, you know how these young people are, especially if they aren't used to living on the frontier."

"You want me to find Charles for you? You know how easily he gets lost out here," Levi offered, picking up his bow and quiver.

"You do that boy," said John. "It's high time he came back and cooked supper."

Levi picked up Charity's bow and quiver and walked out of the camp, half expecting Samson Wallace to call him back. He saw Charity hidden in the midst of several big trees, watching him. He casually dropped her bow and quiver and kept on walking.

Still in sight of Wallace, he circled the site, watching for men hiding in the thick foliage. Just as he turned to go back, an arm gripped him around the waist. At the same time a grimy hand covered his mouth, and he was marched into camp.

Seeing Levi held captive by Indians, John lifted his rifle only to lose it to Samson Wallace.

"I don't see how you've lasted this long in these mountains. You're a damned fool to pack like this with only two boys for help," he said. "You've been lucky so far, but your good luck just ran out. Tie them up."

"So, after welcoming you to our camp, you betray us like this?"

"But of course. We do what we please, and we take from anyone we please. Besides, my men didn't appreciate it when you killed those young braves back there. Since you didn't scalp them, they knew you were white and from your tracks, heavily laden with goods. That's all it took to make them determined to chase you to the gates of hell."

"I guess it doesn't matter that they were intent on robbing and killing us," said John, trying to appear calm, and hoping Charity would stay hidden. "What do you intend to do with us now?"

"I see no reason to kill you since we can use you to carry these packs back to our village. After that…, who knows?" He looked at Levi, an evil grin on his face. "These six men and those you killed were very close. Some were kin, and you know what that means."

John was afraid Levi would be scared, but the boy showed no sign of it, instead, Levi caught John's eye. In total silence, without moving a muscle, the shared message was, save Charity.

Charity watched the drama from her vantage point with her heart in her mouth. She studied the situation in the camp and formulated plans for a rescue, but none of them seemed feasible. As the sun dipped behind the mountain, she remained in the dark shadows with bow and quiver, waiting for the right opportunity.

Wallace's men tied John and Levi to trees on opposite sides of the camp with straps pulling their hands up above them. They took the rabbits and a turkey Levi and Charity shot earlier and set them to roast on a spit. Wallace pulled out a jug and shared it with the Indians.

Charity's stomach growled in response to the scent of roasting meat as she watched the men eat their fill. Ravenous, she took a chunk of dried meat from the pouch on her belt and gnawed on it, trying to figure out a way to save herself and her companions.

The band settled down for the night after a few nips from the jug, and they posted only one guard. The guard's belly was full and firewater dulled his senses, so he leaned back against a tree, facing the fire. That meant his vision would be seconds coming into focus in the darkness. He stared into the fire until his head began to bob up and down. He caught himself and began to blink, his eyes taking longer to open each time. When he finally nodded off and his mouth fell open, Charity saw her chance.

She sighted on the rawhide holding John's hands above his head, said a little prayer, and sent an arrow flying.

John, who was trying to keep the straps from cutting the blood off from his hands, heard the arrow thud into the leather binding him. He knew who shot the arrow; no one but Charity would attempt such a shot in the flickering firelight. In silence, he sawed the strap back and forth until it snapped.

Charity watched until John's strap broke free of the tree, and then shot the leather binding Levi. The guard roused, alerted by the thud of the arrow, but before he could sound the alarm, Charity shot another arrow into his chest. His head fell forward, and he appeared to be asleep with an arrow pinning him to the tree.

With great stealth, John and Levi lifted their packs, retrieved their weapons, and slipped out of camp undetected.

"Let's get far from here," John whispered. "Take off your moccasins and we'll walk in the stream to confuse them. Those braves are pretty young. They may not be as good at tracking as older warriors would be. I hope Wallace lets the braves do the tracking. I figure we have until dawn to get as far from here as possible."

They walked barefoot in the cold water through the night, their feet numb, looking for a place to take shelter. When John saw a large slab of limestone that had landed on its side at the water's edge, he led them to it saying, "We'll rest here and get some sleep. Even Indians can't track footprints in a stream in the dark, and we need all the rest we can get."

Levi and Charity settled into the back corner of the overhang and went straight to sleep. John, however, couldn't sleep as he weighed the chances of escape against Wallace's pending assault. When he finally lay down to sleep, the problem was still on his mind.

As the sun rose the next morning, they began to assess the situation. "We can't assume Wallace won't follow us," John told them. "He must do so to save face. If not, his men will leave him, and he will lose status among them. Or, they may kill him for letting us get away with their plunder. God knows, they are ruthless enough."

"What you are saying is if we don't kill them all when they attack, we'll never have a single night's peace for the rest of the trip, and we'll always be looking over our shoulders to see who's back there," said Charity. "I say we should rest for now and wait for them here. This valley is very narrow, and if we hide on both sides, we could catch them in a cross fire like we did before."

The men agreed with her strategy, and they devised their plan. "Charity, Darlin', you stay up here," said John. "Levi, you climb behind those rocks on that side, and I'll hide behind that outcropping in front. String your bows and make sure you have plenty of arrows ready. Now, let's get in position; they should be getting close."

They all checked their bowstrings to make sure they weren't frayed, checked the arrows and divided them evenly, and took their places as the sun rose high in the sky. Flies buzzed around them, and ants crawled over them. Birds flew up to their rocks, but they sat so still they didn't scare them and give away their positions.

Charity was settled into position when she saw the Indians slipping down the stream, carefully watching both sides for ambush. As before, Samson Wallace walked in the safest spot—in the middle of his men.

When the sixth warrior passed her, Charity stood in the shadows, arrow notched and ready to shoot. She waited until she saw Levi do the same. Their arrows flew at the same time, and two men fell in the water while the remaining four panicked, looking for the hidden archers. John's arrow hit a third man, and Levi and Charity took the other two out, leaving Samson Wallace the only one left alive.

"I give up, don't shoot," he said. Carefully, the man put his rifle down on a rock, raised his hands, and began to walk toward John.

John and Levi walked forward, their bows ready, but Charity stayed where she was, watching. She didn't trust Wallace, a man who killed both Indians and whites with impunity.

John and Levi were about a dozen feet from Wallace when he dropped his hands. Before they could take cover, he pulled two pistols from his belt, cocked and ready, and aimed directly at them. Before Wallace could shoot, however, he collapsed where he stood, an arrow from Charity's bow through his heart.

"Thanks, Darlin'. I didn't even suspect he had pistols under his coat. Levi and I are lucky you were watching."

Charity turned pale. "What if I had missed?"

"But you didn't, remember that." Picking up Samson's rifle, he handed it to Levi. "Here, Levi, you now have your own rifle. We'll take his shot and his pistols, also.

Finding multiple footprints on the path they intended to take, John set a fast pace and kept them in the stream all day. During the night, they alternated the watch, and John reminded them to be cautious of every sound.

Two days later they stopped to study their back trail. "My gut tells me we're being followed again. There's a cave up that side canyon where a lone hunter once holed up for days. The Indians never found him, and he lived to tell the tale. He told me about it and said it was so well hidden even the Indians weren't aware of it. We need to find the cave and quickly. Keep your eyes open and watch for anything unusual in the cliffs above us."

The group followed the small canyon. Its walls had been sculpted by wind and water. They explored, looking for the cave. Gigantic boulders balanced precariously on pinnacles of stone, sand, and gravel. The silence was deafening as they made their way between the towering ramparts of stone, wary of the rocks overhead.

"Look. Up there," Charity whispered. "See that large boulder up near the top, the one lodged against a tree? I saw a fox run behind the boulder, and he didn't come out the other side. Maybe the cave is there, behind that boulder."

"Or, she may have only a small den behind the boulder," John said. "You and Levi keep watch while I check it out."

"Not on your life," Charity told him, gripping his hand in hers. "If there's a cave up there, we'll all find it and be there together. I don't like being separated with Indians chasing us in this canyon."

After a long grueling climb, they reached the boulder. "That's it. You found it, you brilliant woman," John said, giving her a hug. "Come on, let's get inside before they see us." The entrance was so small they had to bend over to get in, but once inside, they found the cavern was huge.

"No wonder the hunter wasn't found. He had the perfect place to hide," said Levi. "He could have stood off an army from here, but what I want to know is what happened to the fox?"

"The tracks run around to the back," said John, pointing down. I'll bet there's a back exit somewhere, and the fox knows where it is. Either that, or it will slip out this way while we sleep. We have a good field of vision from here, and we can see both up and down the canyon. Put your packs down and relax."

"How long do you think we'll have to stay here?" Levi looked around inside the cave.

"With the food we took off those young Indians and with our own supply, we have enough for several days, but if we have to we could stay longer. Being hungry is better than being dead. There's a small seep in the back for water. From the looks of the soot on the ceiling back there, smoke must filter out."

"The idea of laying around for a couple of days sounds good to me, and I could use some sleep," said Charity, dropping her pack to the floor of the cave.

John kissed her when she straightened up and said, "We can sleep as late as we want in the morning, providing those Indians don't find us."

Glad for a chance to rest, they ate jerky for supper and crawled into blankets for much needed rest.

When dawn finally came, heavy clouds hung low over the canyon. Below, a party of Indians scoured the canyon floor for footprints, but when the rain came, torrents of water crashed down over the rocks, obliterating the tracks.

A bolt of lightning shot across the sky, shattering a tree nearby. When thunder rumbled overhead, echoing up and down the canyon walls, the Indians turned back, knowing too well how easily avalanches start on such steep walls, but it was already too late.

A trickle of gravel slid lazily down from the top, dropping ledge to ledge, picking up speed and more rock as it went until the canyon wall fell apart. The Indians, already running for their lives, tripped and fell under the assault until there were more wounded than there were men to help.

One warrior shook his fist back at the canyon yelling, "Place of Evil Spirits," as he ran.

"What did he say?" Levi asked John.

"He named the canyon, Place of Evil Spirits." They'll probably avoid it from now on. Any place that causes so much damage to their people is evil in their minds. We all avoid places where we've been hurt."

"Does this mean we can rest without the fear of being murdered in our sleep?" Charity watched from the overhanging shelter as light rain changed to heavy rain and wondered what more could go wrong. They still had one another, but the challenges were piling up fast.

They built a small fire in the back of the cave from sticks that littered the shelf in front of the cave's entrance. It was dark back there, but as John said, paying attention to the smallest details of their safety, "I'd rather be vigilant and keep my hair."

Looking at John's hair in the firelight, Charity thought he really did have nice hair; hair she enjoyed running her fingers through…. She chuckled under her breath; it was almost comical to think about how her opinion of him had changed during their journey over the mountains. Once she thought John Mason was an evil, mean-spirited man, and one she would have gladly killed, but now she loved him dearly.

After several hours with nothing to do, Levi grew restless, pacing around the cave until he finally said, "John, I think I'll take a torch and follow those fox tracks. I'm tired of sitting around. I used to explore caves near my home when I was a kid. I love searching through them. Can you do without me for a while?"

"That's a good idea, but take this chalk rock and an extra torch so when the cave branches, you can mark your trail and find your way back."

As the light of Levi's torch receded in the dark tunnel, John shook out their blankets and moved them further from the entrance. He caught Charity staring at him and asked, "Why are you looking at me that way?"

"What way? Can't I look at the man I love?" she said, admiring his body, licentious thoughts racing through her head.

"And what were you thinking while you were looking at me like that?" he asked, kneeling on one knee beside her.

"Come on, what were you thinking?" He lifted her chin with his finger, brushing her lips with his. "Were you thinking you wanted me to do this?"

"Oh, you stir so many feelings in me," she said, gently caressing his face. "I can't keep my eyes off you, and when I look into your eyes, it feels like I'm swimming in them." Touching a lock of his hair, she continued, "The sun shines on your hair, and I want to run my fingers through it. I watch your lips and want to feel them on mine. Is that what you want to hear?"

"That will do for now," he said, looking deeply into her eyes. "I want to kiss you until you gasp for breath, and much more, but I'd be taking advantage of the situation, and I can't do that to you, even though I want to. I just can't dishonor you."

He kissed her again and reluctantly stood up, turning away to get himself under control. Finding it more difficult than he thought it would be, he left her by the fire and stood outside in the rain to cool down.

Charity watched him leave the cave with longing. Excited by the feelings he roused in her, she was restless. But she had only a vague idea of what would satisfy her desire.

It was still raining when Charity awoke the next morning in a quandary. She needed to relieve her bladder after the long night. She stood at the cave's entrance, her legs held close together.

Should she go out in the pouring rain to relieve herself, one hand holding her pants, the other gripping a rock to keep her balance? One misstep on the rain-slick ledge and she would go sliding, bare-bottom, down the limestone cliff.

The image didn't appeal to her.

Levi saw her hesitation and asked, "What's wrong, Charity? Why don't you go outside to relieve yourself?"

She turned back to him and said, "It's a bit more difficult for me than it is for you, Levi. I have to practically get undressed."

"Sure, but…. Hey, when I was exploring last night, I found where the trapped hunter relieved himself. It's way back there in a tiny room. There are a lot of cave rooms back there, and it's no wonder the Indians never found him. He had everything he needed up here, and no reason to come out. Come on, I'll show you where it is. I marked it with the chalk rock so it would be easy to find. It's off to the side by itself, so don't worry, you'll have plenty of privacy."

"Indians can track by scent, too," said John. You and I will need to use that room ourselves while we are holed up here. Right now, the rain is washing ours away but we need to be more cautious."

Charity and John sorted through the food supplies while Levi kept first watch. The leather bags from the Indians contained foodstuffs new to her.

"I've never seen meal like this before, and look at this, it's some kind of dried fruit patty. So do you know what they are?"

"This is dried persimmon, those are dried mulberries. They're good energy food for long hunts or on the warpath. The women roll them in cornmeal and fry them in bear grease. That meal is made from ground white corn, dried beans, and potatoes, and it makes excellent bread. I still have some bear grease left, so we can have good bread this morning with our boiled jerky and a dried mulberry patty for dessert."

Using the bear grease John kept in a small tin, they fried the bread mixture on a flat rock in the fire, browning the bread lightly on each side.

"We haven't eaten this well in weeks. Maybe when we get to the Cherokee village someone will teach me how to cook like this."

I'm surprised you want to learn Indian ways," John said. "You won't need them when you go back east."

"But, I do want to know. I have a lot to learn and knowing this will make me a better cook, anywhere I may live," she replied. Besides, I didn't realize Indians ate so well, and I didn't know they had so much variety. I thought they only ate venison and corn."

Nodding, John agreed. "Did you try to eat the food back in Mud Flat? It was bad, and as drunk as I was, even I noticed the difference. From my experience, the Cherokee have a varied diet and use even more wild plants for seasoning. They eat a wide selection of greens, some we don't think of as being edible, and they have more varieties of corn than we do."

"Wild onions and carrots mixed in the batter would be good in this bread batter too and make it go further. From now on let's keep watch for them on the trail. For right now, I'm going to divide the flour and dried cakes so we can have some each day while it lasts. Then it will be back to jerky and cornmeal mush again."

Charity's next question burned her throat as she voiced it. "Are you going back, or are you going to stay with the Indians?"

John stared at her in surprise. His intention had been to stay with the Cherokee one or two years, collecting a fortune in furs and to return a wealthy man. Already close to his goal, he would have all the prime furs he could carry by spring if they reached the village. Now, having met Charity, he didn't know what to do.

He walked to the entrance and stood there, staring at the vast, rain-soaked, clean-smelling, mountainous landscape. No sooty smoke clouded the air, no rutted roads scarred the land, and there were no sounds of pigs and cattle. The only sounds were those of rain splattering against the rocks.

Charity watched his reverie without speaking. She was aware of how much he enjoyed the freedom of being out in wild untamed land far away from settlements. She also knew making a decision about a future, that might never come, could wait.

She decided to change the subject. "Do you think it will rain long?"

He turned back toward her. "I can't see the horizon from here, it's raining too hard. We'll have to stay put until it quits, unless you like the idea of walking all day, soaking wet."

"I vote to stay high and dry until the rain stops," quipped Levi. "If we hadn't found a safe, dry place to camp, we'd be sleeping in wet clothes in the rain and mud."

John agreed, "We still have plenty of wood for the fire, but we need to use it only for cooking and then douse it. I don't want the smell of smoke drifting into the fresh air. My gut tells me those Indians are still around, and if they smell smoke, they'll know we're still here."

As a result, they stayed where they were, waiting it out, and after three days, the rain let up. Torrents of water that had gushed down the canyon slowed to a trickle and stopped altogether.

The three of them stood near the entrance, looking out on the scene below. The air was clean. Pines clinging precariously to the canyon's walls swayed in the breeze; evergreen scent drifted into the cave. John sniffed the air like an animal in its native habitat.

Charity watched him, thinking how free and alive he looked. How would he handle the restrictions of civilization if he went back east? Would he miss the clean air, the freedom, and the thrill of living on the edge? She tried to imagine him in topcoat, pantaloons, and stiff buckled shoes, talking politics or the latest news with the other men and couldn't do it. She would always remember him in buckskins like he was this day, watching the horizon, senses alert, trusting his instincts to warn him of danger.

Sniffing the air, John looked up behind them to see smoke drifting out the entrance instead of the smoke hole. He moved quickly and whispered, "Smoke. Douse the fire, now!"

"Now I know why my nerves were on edge," he said quietly. "Those Indians saw or smelled smoke back up there and plugged the hole. They're waiting for it to show them exactly where we are."

"I knew I should have scalped those seven braves we killed. By not scalping them, we told everyone we're whites, and that means plunder or captives in their book. Now that they know where we are, they'll never let up, and any movement we make will bring them down on us. We have to come up with a plan."

"I saw Charity's face when I scalped the first one. She looked at me like I was disgusting. It made my stomach turn, and I didn't want to see that expression again. Just look at everything that's happened since I made that decision. Samson and his group caught us, now we're trapped in this cave while the others hover around waiting for us to make our move."

"Oh John, I'm so sorry. I was pretending to be Charles then, or I might have said something. I didn't think you were disgusting. I was disgusted at what you had to do. So now, I've put us in danger by being so squeamish." Thinking if she hadn't betrayed her emotions on her face, they might not be in this position!

"It's not your fault, darlin'. Traveling through these parts was bound to be dangerous from the start. We've been lucky to have you on this journey; we wouldn't have survived Samson's attack without you. These problems may just be coincidental. The point is, that it is happening and we know they're watching the canyon now."

"When I went exploring in the caves," Levi told them. "I saw where the fox got out, but it's too small for us to crawl through. It's way back past where the smoke used to go out. This entrance is the only way in or out."

Taking turns watching for movement below, they ate jerky for supper without lighting a fire and went to bed. The next morning, they again chewed jerky and shared a persimmon patty while considering the situation they were in.

Finally, Charity spoke. "John, those men are exceptional trackers, and surely by now, they know I'm a woman, yes?"

"Most likely they've got you figured for a woman. What are you thinking?"

"The way I see it is, we have two options: first, we can sit up here and hope they give up and go away, which isn't likely. They probably know we don't have much food with us, even if we have water, so they may decide to sit down there and wait while we grow weaker by the day. Have I assessed the situation correctly?"

By the look in John's eyes, Charity knew he didn't like the direction she was going, but she continued. "Second, we're trapped here. Let's take the battle to them; use our wits against them. We need to provide a diversion. Since they know I'm a woman, if they see me leave the cave, they'll most likely follow me. I would be a prize catch wouldn't I, and whoever caught me would own me, right?"

Images playing through his mind of Charity caught by the Indians, John held up his hand, stopping her. "That's the way they work, but I don't even want to hear the rest of it. Forget it."

"John, put yourself in their place for a minute. They have no idea there's a primitive bathroom in these caves. It will look like I'm an inexperienced white woman foolishly going out to relieve herself in privacy since the rain has stopped. They'll probably figure they can easily capture me and get you two later."

Levi, who had said little up to this point, agreed with Charity. "John, if you and I are hidden behind the boulder in front of the cave's entrance, we will have them in view when they come out to get Charity, but they won't be able to see us. All they will see is Charity slipping away, so I think it might work."

"No. I will not risk her life just to save ours, and that's what it might come down to," he said with abject fear on his strong face. "We don't know how many there are. There could be dozens of them and we can't possibly kill them all.

Charity, falling in love with John Mason all over again, wrapped her arms around him while he composed himself. Taking a deep breath, he turned around and took her in his arms, his heart pounding next to hers.

"I don't like the idea of you being a decoy with Levi and me expected to kill anyone following you. I'd rather stay here and starve to death with you, before putting you in danger," he declared. "It's so risky it petrifies me, but in the absence of a better plan, I guess we'd better consider it."

Charity took her hair down and combed the braids out, leaving it to hang loose down her back, dusted her leathers free of debris and prepared to leave.

Had John seen the delicate way she combed through her golden locks before she left, his resolve might have crumbled, but he was intent on the Indians down below.

With supposed stealth, she crept out of the cave and pretended to look for a spot to do her business. Looking back, as though insuring her privacy, she tugged at the tie on her leather pants, golden curls shining bright around her shoulders. Not once did she glance down where the Indians were hiding.

John and Levi set up on each side of the boulder. When an Indian appeared only a dozen feet away from where Charity struggled with her ties, John notched an arrow and in one fluid movement let it fly. The arrow bounced off the ledge and hit the man in the throat.

Levi spotted yet another Indian rising from a dip in the ground and loosed an arrow, hitting the man in the chest. Charity failed to hear them fall and continued to act as decoy.

John and Levi, searching for movement nearby, were very much aware of how close she had come to capture, but there was no way to tell her to stay down where she was.

As they watched in horror, Charity stood up as though to straighten her clothing, shook that shining head of hair, and began to look around as though lost.

Seeing her walk into the open, two warriors gave chase. A volley of arrows struck them both down within yards of where she stood. Hearing them fall, Charity turned, gripping her knife. When yet another man leapt at her, she plunged her knife deep into the warm body. Surprised, he grunted, staring down at seven inches of steel protruding from his stomach. Falling, he took her down with him.

Blood spurted on the ground, mixing with rainwater, as Charity struggled to get out from underneath the warrior's dead weight. She yanked the knife from him, scrambled to her feet and stood ready for another attack.

Hearing footsteps pounding toward her, she crouched, ready to strike as two men charged forward. Recognizing John and Levi who were panting from the frantic race to save her, she drew back.

Seeing the warrior's blood pooled on the ground at her feet, John took Charity in his arms. "You're hurt!" he cried. "Levi, help me, we've got to tend her wounds."

John's face was white and his hands were shaking, as he pulled her leather shirt up, searching for the wound. Charity pushed him away, and pointing to the dead man at her feet said, "John, pull my shirt down, I'm not hurt. That's his blood, not mine!"

After making sure all members of the war party were either dead or fleeing, they sat down to take stock of the situation, one on either side of Charity. She hugged both men as reality sunk in; they had beaten the odds once again.

"Let's get out of here," John said after catching his breath. "I don't think this canyon is a healthy place for us anymore. Those Indians know we are here, and they'll be back with reinforcements."

Ignoring exhaustion, they climbed back to the cave, took their packs, and stripped the dead warriors of valuables on the way back down. Levi found where the Indians had stashed their food supplies. They took the food, too, and left the canyon behind.

As the land leveled out, they put distance between themselves and the canyon before stopping for the night. Lying down under the stars, all three found it difficult to sleep at first. Earlier in the day, after the band of Indians discovered their hiding place, they had escaped from what they thought of as safe refuge. They had made and implemented a plan, using Charity as a decoy, and they had succeeded without a single scratch. Now, no longer in hiding in the darkness of the cave, they were in the open with the moon shining above.

Before falling asleep, Charity watched John for a few minutes, longing to be next to him. Memories, of the time he rescued her after she fell in the river and took a chill, flooded her mind. She fantasized about his naked body gleaming in the campfire, and how that night, he'd slept in the nude next to her own bare body to give them both warmth. She recalled how his breath felt on the back of her neck, his arm draped over her body, and it made her want him.

The next day was blessedly uneventful with no Indians in sight. The three companions followed a stream warmed by the sun to a small waterfall, at the base of which was a small pool, and set up camp.

When Charity announced her intention to bathe in the pool, John found a root next to the stream bank and gave it to her saying, "Here, use this soap weed root for your bath. Just crush it and use the sap."

Charity took the root, leisurely undressed near the waterfall, and slid into the warm water tumbling into the pool to bathe. The little pond was so pleasant that she allowed herself to sink until only her face was above water, enjoying the luxury of it.

Hearing voices, she assumed John and Levi decided to bathe. Gliding soundlessly to the waterfall, she found a place to crouch behind the falling water and peered through the mist to find them. Instead of their familiar voices, she heard a woman's laughter and the voice of a man.

Thinking her clothes were in plain sight, she held her breath as an Indian couple swam toward her, splashing and dunking each other. When the man grabbed the woman and fondled her breasts, holding her tight against his nakedness, his erection rubbing against the girl's buttocks, Charity's virgin heart skipped a beat.

A voyeur that day, she observed their sexual foreplay in the water with only a vague idea of what lovemaking was between a man and a woman. When they climbed out to lie on the soft, green grass and made love, she got the education she yearned for.

While she felt guilty watching them, she could not stop. Their passionate kisses and excited bodies, joined in a tangle of arms and legs, fascinated her. The woman's pleasure as the man caressed her in forbidden places was entrancing.

He took his time with the woman, and when she was ready, entered her body with practiced ease, eliciting groans from them both. Their lovemaking seemed to go on forever, but at last, his motion sped up, and with a cry, he emptied himself into the woman, smothering her scream of pleasure with his mouth.

When at last they lay still, holding one another and talking softly, Charity was both embarrassed and stimulated by the couple and wanted the experience for herself. Dazed by what she had just seen, she waited a while after the couple left giggling and holding hands. She then swam to the other side of the pool to her clothes.

Approaching the camp, John grabbed her saying, "We were scared out of our minds. We saw fresh tracks, heard voices, and tried to signal you, but you were sunk so low in the water you couldn't see us. We saw you go behind the waterfall, so we felt you were safe. Why did you take so long to come out?"

"There were some Indians swimming near the waterfall, and I couldn't get past them," she replied. "I assumed you knew they were there, too, as you and Levi promised to keep watch."

In truth, her body tingling at what she had seen, she wasn't about to admit to John Mason she stayed to watch a couple make love in the grass, but she thought about it a lot in the coming days.

Chapter 7

Traveling across unnamed ridges and valleys only the Indians knew, the scene back at the waterfall replayed in Charity's mind repeatedly. Afraid lest he see the passion she felt, she kept her head down rather than let John see the pure lust in her eyes.

At night, when they stopped to make camp and he was nearby, all her senses tingled and were fully aware of him. She wondered what it would have been like if it had been the two of them at the waterfall. She wanted to run her hands over his broad chest, kiss him, and have him make love to her just the way the Indian man did with his woman.

One moonlit night, as they sat on a log near a stream to watch shooting stars, John put his arm around her shoulders, holding her close without speaking. Finally, when she could stand it no more, Charity broke the silence.

"John, I love you, and I know you love me, but do you want me as a lover?"

"Want you as only a lover? What would make you think such a thing?" he said, hugging her. "If you were just my lover, you might find another someday."

"Well, you never asked me to marry you, but I thought that surely if you cared, you'd at least want to make love to me."

John shook his head, staring at the woman in the moonlight, images of her in his bed dancing through his mind. That she would want to marry him never crossed his mind, until that moment. *Of course, I want to marry this woman. How could I not? Was there ever any other option?*

The realization hit him so hard, that he considered being hit on the head with a boulder would've been a lesser blow.

Charity, insecure already, didn't know what to think of his reaction. Fighting tears, she rose, but he caught her hand and drew her back down.

"Why should I take you as a lover when I can marry you and have a wife and a lover?" He got down on one knee and proposed to the woman he loved. "Charity, will you marry me?"

"Are you sure, John? I don't want you to say anything you don't mean. Robert did me that way, and when he left, it hurt. I love you so much that if you left me, I'd die."

"Darlin', you didn't answer my question."

"Yes, I want to marry you. But—"

"But what?" He held his breath, dreading her next words.

"John Mason, I've found the man I want, and I want him now. Tonight. I don't want to wait any longer."

"You are so full of surprises." He said, taking her into his arms. "Do you really want to marry me that quickly? No second thoughts? No doubts?"

"I would marry you tonight if I could."

"Would you be happy with my heartfelt pledge to you, and yours to me? I've heard of frontier people joining like that, sometimes under the full moon. They seem to be happy with such a marriage."

"When is the moon full again?

"Look up, darlin'. It's full tonight.

"Oh, John, go get Levi, let him witness our pledging on this beautiful night. I'll wait here for you."

John left in such a hurry he stumbled and fell face down in soft sand. Reaching camp with dirt on his face and his hair in disarray, he grabbed Levi by the hand and dragged him back to where Charity waited.

"What's wrong, John? Can't you tell me anything?" But John refused to stop long enough to give him an answer.

Charity waited for the men, pondering the best words to bind them together. It was her wedding night, and she was overflowing with happiness. When John and Levi burst through the woods, breathing hard, they found her sitting on the log, grinning.

Relieved to see Charity was neither missing nor hurt, Levi looked around to see what was wrong. After catching his breath, John explained why they needed him, and suddenly, everything fell into place; they wanted him to witness their joining.

John found a little cove where the moon found entrance, cleared it of debris, and turned to Charity who looked at him strangely. "John, why do you have dirt all over your face?"

"I was in such a hurry to get Levi that I fell," he said with a sheepish grin. "I didn't want you to have time to change your mind."

He stared in wonder as she wet her hands in the stream and then cleaned his face and combed his hair with her fingers. This beautiful woman, bathed in moonlight, agreed to be his wife.

John's mind went blank as they stood in the moon's silver beam. What does a man, with no experience at weddings, say as a marriage vow?

Charity, seeing his expression, smiled and pulled his hand to her heart and pressed it there. Her eyes bright in the moonlight, she gazed into his eyes and recited from memory, "I take thee, John Mason, as my chosen husband, to love and cherish, from this day forward, and until death do us part."

Still holding his hand on her heart, John gave his vow. "I take you, Charity, to be my wife from this day forward, to love you and care for you until the end of my days."

***

Watching them with a jubilant grin, Levi whispered, "At last." The two turned toward him expectantly. Performing his solemn role in the wedding, he straightened up, trying to look official and said, "I declare under God that I've witnessed these two declare their love and vow to be married. You may kiss the bride."

The last was unnecessary, as they were already kissing and had forgotten about him. Realizing the task was finished, Levi walked back to camp. On his return he stated out loud, "I didn't do too badly for a seventeen…, no, eighteen-year-old who's never seen a wedding before.

When he reached camp, Levi began a surprise for Charity and John. Working quickly he laid fresh pine boughs on the ground to create a soft mattress and spread their ground sheets and blankets over it. After scratching a note in the dirt by the bed, he took his own bedding and some food to the trailhead to keep watch. They needed no surprises on their wedding night.

Intending to find a secluded place to spend their first night together, John and Charity walked back to camp, hand in hand, to grab their blankets. Instead, they found their wedding bed made and Levi missing. Momentary panic filled both until John found a note scratched in the sand. "It says, 'gone fishing for three days. Happy Honeymoon.'"

"He's a good man, I hope we can do the same for him sometime."

John took Charity in his arms and between kisses said, "Mrs. Mason, would you care to join me on our wedding bed?"

His kisses were so intoxicating Charity had trouble finding her voice, but with a coy look from under her lashes, she finally said. "Mr. Mason, my clothes seem terribly uncomfortable right now, would you like to help me take them off?"

As though in a worshipful trance, John slowly lifted the buckskin shirt away from her creamy skin. Setting her luscious breasts free so distracted him that his fingers fumbled with the knot holding her trousers. Anxious herself, she helped him and soon, her pants followed the shirt to the ground.

He begun to undress when she nuzzled the hair on his chest and said, "You don't have to run and hide behind a tree for relief tonight, Mr. Mason, darling."

"You knew. I thought you were asleep when I caressed you!" Sliding his hands down to her enticing buttocks, he pulled her close.

"No, I wasn't asleep," she said between kisses.

"But you didn't move or slap my hands away," he said, holding her tight.

"Why should I? Until then, I didn't know what passion felt like, and I didn't want you to stop anyway. Now you can teach me what my body longed for then," she said, running her fingertips through the hair on his chest.

Taking his time, he nuzzled her neck, kissed along her jaw, and then finally, her delicate throat, saying, "That could take a while you know, maybe a lifetime."

"In that case, hadn't we better get started?" she said, almost purring under his touch. She gasped when he sucked blood to the surface of her shoulder.

"I love you," he told her, his voice husky with passion.

When John awoke in the night, it was to find his hand on her breast as though it had a right to be there. He pulled back, and then remembered the vows they had taken. He slid his hand back around to find his favorite handhold and cuddled it gently.

Charity sighed, put her hand over his, and backed her naked body closer, murmuring, "Don't do that if you're only teasing. You already know what that does to me."

The sultry comment was enough to bring John fully awake and fully aroused. He was not teasing. He rolled her on her back, continuing his massage with both hands. When he took her full breast in his mouth, she was suddenly awake and fully alert. "I warned you," she told him, pulling him to her willing body.

It was late morning when they woke, ravenous. Alone in the wilderness, neither bothered with clothing as they prepared to eat. Seeing a nude Charity bent over their foodstuff, John forgot about food and decided he wanted her instead. By the time they finally got around to eating, they were starving.

John watched Charity eat the last of the mulberry patties, her every move an enchantment for him. His eyes roamed over her toned, healthy young body and again, his interest turned from nourishment to her. My stomach can wait, he decided, my desire for her can't.

On the fourth day, they woke, stomachs growling, to find Levi sitting by the fire, grilling a string of fish and with a turkey roasting on a spit fashioned from a stick. The smell of food was heavenly.

"Good morning," Levi said, his face discreetly turned from them. "I have breakfast cooking in case anyone's hungry."

Charity snuggled closer to John and whispered in his ear. "Do you remember where my clothes are? I don't see them anywhere."

"You haven't needed them lately, have you?" he responded with a grin. "Let me get up. I'll find them for you."

"Hurry, my bladder is full," she whispered. "I can't get up and walk around naked like I've been doing."

"If you're wondering where your clothes are; they're over here in a pile." Levi said politely. "I'll hand them to you." Handing them the clothes, he continued, "I decided to let you have another day, but I've seen a lot of smoke off in the distance and it's too big for a campfire. It's either a wildfire or a village burning. I thought you'd want to know, because we may need to get out of here pretty soon.

They ate as much fish and turkey as they wanted, along with some of the Indian bread and the remaining persimmon patty.

Watching John and Charity consume breakfast, Levi asked, "Didn't you two eat for the last three days?"

"Oh, we snacked off and on, but neither of us felt like cooking much," John said, cutting his eyes toward Charity, who, remembering why they neglected to eat, dropped her head to hide a blush.

"Thanks for the breakfast, Levi. It was nice of you," Charity said, kissing his cheek.

Blushing bright red he replied, "You're welcome. You two are my only family now, so I have to take care of you."

"You and I are in the same boat, Levi," she responded. "I have no family left back home either, so John is my only family now." Then she surprised the young man by asking, "I've always wanted a brother. Levi, would you like to be my little brother?"

"I'd like that." He looked thoughtful for a moment, and he grinned at her saying, "Will that make John my brother-in-law?"

"I hadn't thought about it, but I guess so," Charity said with an easy laugh. "How funny it is that I came on this journey to find my fiancé and have ended up with a new husband and a brother."

"That's all the more reason for me to look after you two. We're supposed to take care of family. It's a relief to know you still want me along. I was afraid you might not and that I might be in your way."

"Levi, we need you now more than ever. You've already proven your value to us. Surely three sets of eyes are better when we travel. Besides, I seem to be distracted these days," said John, watching Charity tie up her bedroll and load her backpack. "I will need you around more than ever to help keep us from getting killed."

The next day they found the source of the smoke. Reaching a peak, they stared into the charred remains of a village. Surveying the site, John told them, "It takes a large force to take over a village this size. This must be what Samson Wallace meant when he said the French were stirring up tribes to attack Indians friendly to the English."

Avoiding the carnage, they continued over the next mountain range for several days until they came to a Cherokee village. While it appeared to be peaceful, they approached with caution, John going so far as to tie a scalp to the fringe of Levi's shirt. "This shows he's a warrior," he said in response to Charity's puzzled expression. "It will get him respect."

As they approached the peaceful community, John warned Charity and Levi against sudden moves or drawing their weapons. "We're being followed, so just stay calm. I know these people—they are friendly—but they might not respond well to an aggressive move."

The Peace Chief, who knew John, welcomed them warmly. As he led them to the circle by the fire, dogs barked, children raced by, and all of the women stared at Charity.

"Why do they look at me like that, John?"

"It's your hair."

"What do you mean by, 'It's my hair?' Do they want my hair and are they going to scalp me for it?"

"No, darlin', they've never seen long, blonde hair before. You are the envy of the womenfolk."

Smiling at that, she retorted, "We'll get along just fine as long as they don't try to take it from me. I'm partial to having it on my head."

Levi's dangling scalp drew attention as some of the people, including the younger women, noticed it hanging from his fringe.

As they reached the village plaza where a group had gathered, a tall man, his expression stern, strode forward to greet John. It was Robert, Charity's former fiancé.

The men clasped hands briefly and stood back, staring at each other, until Robert broke the silence, saying, "I see you've returned with heavy packs to use for Gray Dove's dowry, well you are too late. I loved her too much to risk you out bidding me for her hand, and she returned my affection. We joined over her father's objections, and she is now my wife."

To Robert's surprise, John grinned and pulled Charity around to his side and introduced her. "Robert, I want you to meet my wife, Charity Mason, your former fiancé."

Staring at Charity, Robert's face turned ashen. Even dressed as a boy, he should have recognized the woman standing in front of him.

"Charity, what are you doing here?" Flustered at seeing her, he looked at Gray Dove, then back at Charity. "I'm sorry I ran out on you. I was a coward. I knew I didn't love you, I just couldn't tell you that. Forgive me. You didn't come all this way to get me back, did you?" He looked from John to Charity. "Wait a minute, did you say 'wife'?"

"Yes Robert, he said 'wife.' I am now Mrs. John Mason, thanks to you. While it hurt me terribly when you abandoned both your father, and me, you did me a favor by running away. I thank you for it now, because we would never have been happy. We weren't in love; we were doing what was expected of us. Besides that, I never loved you the way I love John."

"By all that's holy! I'm in shock. To find that you made it through Indians buzzing around like hornets, and you did it with Charity along, and you didn't lose your hair or your packs. This is amazing. Come, let's go to our lodge so we can talk."

Charity took control of the situation saying, "Before we go any further, I'd like to introduce you all to Levi, my adopted brother. Levi, meet Robert, my former fiancé and the man who made it possible for us to meet, and Gray Dove, his wife."

When Levi stepped forward to shake hands, Charity noticed how tall and strong he had grown on their journey, but she wasn't the only one. Some village women watched his every move with admiration in their downcast eyes.

They entered Robert and Gray Dove's lodge. He invited them to sit on the bed along one wall, held off the ground with stout forked tree limbs. He and Gray Dove offered drinks of cool, spring water from gourds sitting in a corner.

Charity looking around at the woven mats on the floor and the reed mats in different colors decorating the walls. She sank on the bed and sighed.

"A soft bed. It's been months since I slept on a soft bed. I'm in heaven,"

Gray Dove gave her an appreciative smile. "I worked very hard to make the bed as soft as that. It is covered with buffalo skins dressed very carefully. I'm glad you like it."

"I love it. You have a beautiful home. I could be very comfortable in one like this." She looked at John, then, she continued, "Robert, I hate to tell you this, but I came all this way to give you the news, and I don't want to prolong it any longer. Your father passed away last year. I'm so sorry."

"I'm not surprised. He told me he only had months to live." He looked down at the floor. "I couldn't face seeing him die." Looking back up at Charity he continued, "Nor could I marry a woman who is more like a sister. It was all too much for me; I was a coward, so I ran away. I left you to take care of my own father after I jilted you. Forgive me. He took a deep breath, "Did Father suffer very much?"

"I wish the doctor had told me what he told your father. It would have helped me understand the way he died. But the doctor never told me it was serious, and neither did your father. I thought it was just from missing you. I hated you for leaving me, but most of all, for leaving him. I had to watch as he just withered away.

"At the reading of the will, I discovered he had made me executor of the estate, and if you failed to return within two years, the property would come to me. Robert, I don't want it. It's yours, but you'll have to go back to claim it."

Gray Dove gasped and turned to Robert.

Charity regretted her words as soon as she saw Gray Dove's reaction. She felt as though Gray Dove was afraid Robert would go back east, leaving her alone. *Stupid! Stupid! Stupid!* she thought and apologized to the woman. "I'm sorry, Gray Dove, I didn't think about how this might affect you. I should have been more discreet. Forgive me."

Robert took Gray Dove in his arms, and holding her tight turned to Charity, "It's amazing what months of open air will do to a man's perspective. I never felt like a real man until I got out here. I love it here, and I love Gray Dove. I don't intend to go back and I don't want the property, inheritance or no," he continued. "I don't want to be a gentleman farmer with my life centered on crops, politics, and gossip, and I don't like living with rules and restrictions on how I should act or dress."

Charity glanced at John, wondering what his response would be to such an announcement. Would he choose to stay in this rugged wilderness, or would he long for the comforts of civilization and return?

***

John, thinking of how to help his friend and partner, broke through her reverie to say, "Robert, didn't you say Gray Dove's father still demands her dowry, even though you've already wed?"

"Oh yes, it will take me all winter to gather enough furs to pay him."

"But, don't you remember, I took some of your furs to sell for you when I left last time?"

Robert hesitated and answered, saying, "No, I don't think so. I still have all of mine."

"You never were any good at accounting," John told him, winking at Charity, "and as usual you are wrong. I sold some of your furs, and I got a good price for them, so that means some of the trade goods we brought are yours. Levi, would you grab your pack, and the one with the extra weapons from those Indians. Those weapons and some trade goods should settle the debt."

***

When the men left, Charity stayed with Gray Dove. They sat quietly, each with questions that needed answers and both hesitant to speak. Finally, Charity broke the ice saying, "Gray Dove, I'm so glad you speak English as my Cherokee isn't good yet. I just wanted to say I'm happy for you and Robert. He deserves a good woman like you."

"Oh, but when I saw your beauty and your golden hair, I was afraid he might forget me," said Gray Dove. "He told me a lot about you, but not how you look. Tell me, do you still love him?"

"Marrying Robert would have been a big mistake for me," Charity responded. "I love him, but it's as a brother. His father wanted us to marry, and I thought I wanted it, too. Thank goodness Robert left when he did, because when I met John, I learned what real love is. What about you? If he had chosen to return to the estate, would you have gone with him?"

Gray Dove looked thoughtful for a moment. "I love him very much, but to go live in a white world, without my family and my tribe around, would have been too hard." she replied. "I fear many would not accept me, and Robert might become ashamed of me. I couldn't stand that, so my answer is, I would stay here."

"I understand. I'm sorry I caused you hurt by telling Robert of his inheritance like that. I am so proud of him for choosing to stay with you. He's brighter than I gave him credit for."

"I will try to keep him as happy as he is right now, and I think I know how, but it's a secret. I haven't told him yet, but I carry his child. If he had chosen to leave, I would never have told him."

"What would you have never told me? Are you keeping secrets from your husband?" Robert asked as he entered, catching only the last sentence. "By the way, your dowry is paid, and you're completely mine. Now, what is this secret you need to tell me?" Sitting next to his wife, Robert pulled her close, waiting for her answer. Gray Dove, blushing, looked down at her feet. Robert lifted her chin with his finger, holding her there until she looked at him.

"I carry your child."

A lightning strike could not have shocked him more. "You wonderful woman! When you agreed to marry me, I thought I could never be happier. But you did it again when you told me we're going to have a son."

"I did not say we would have a son. I said I carry your child, it could be a girl." Gray Dove said, giggling at his excitement.

"I don't care as long as you and the baby are healthy. We can have both for all I care."

Congratulations." John said, slapping Robert on the back, but then Charity saw his expression and knew exactly what he was thinking from the gleam in his eye.

She leaned over to him and whispered, "I know that look very well by now, so quit undressing me with your eyes. We're going to have to find a place of our own where there are no other people around.

Robert broke into their reverie saying, "John, I have all I've ever wanted, a beautiful loving wife and now a child. Now, I want to give you and Charity a wedding present; I give you my father's property. Since I'm staying here, it will belong to Charity in two years anyway, but I want you to have it now. Congratulations John, you married a wealthy woman. I hope you two will be very happy with it."

His words struck Charity, and she reacted heatedly, saying, "If your property was all I wanted, I could have just waited out the two years, after which it would have been mine anyway. I never wanted it, and I won't take it now. It belongs to you and your children. Tell him, John. Tell him we don't want it. John!"

It was obvious John's mind was elsewhere and her words failed to reach him. She glared at him, and failing to get his attention, walked out of the lodge. Her world crashing around her, she found a place to cry. John told her he came here to get enough furs to be rich, now he has his dream. She suspected he would want her to take the property. After all their happiness out here together, learning to rely on their wits and each other, he still might want to go back.

After a while, Charity felt John standing next to her. When she ignored him, he knelt down in front of her and took her in his arms. At first, she struggled against his strength but then gave up and continued crying on his shoulder.

"Honey, Robert's gift took me by surprise. Whether or not we take that property is up to you—it's your right, and I will go where you want to go. I have no right to keep you from a life of ease if that's what you want. I used to want it, too, before I came out here, but I've changed. If we stay here, all I can offer you is the life of an Indian—a lodge with hide-covered beds and hard work—not the big white house on the hill. What do you want?"

"Do you like fancy clothes and tight shoes?"

"No, not since I discovered buckskins and moccasins."

"Do you want people waiting on you hand and foot?"

"No, I only want you waiting for me when I come home."

"Don't you love the freedom to ramble over the country, trusting your gut to keep you safe?"

"You know I love all that, but I love you more. I want what's best for you. If you want to go back, we'll go. If you want to stay here, we'll stay."

"From what I see, these people are living all right. They eat well and look happy and healthy. What's wrong with living like that? John, I love you the way you are. I've discovered I don't like soft, pampered men."

"If you're certain, tell Robert you refuse the property. I was sure you wanted to go back and it broke my heart. I was afraid you would stay just to please me."

"I thought you might be lusting for a life of fancy clothes and powdered wigs. Wouldn't you feel silly wearing a wig?" she asked, wiping her eyes.

John pulled Charity to her feet, and together they walked arm in arm. Robert and Gray Dove stood and Levi held his breath, waiting for their answer.

John cleared his throat and said, "Robert, Charity and I don't want to seem ungracious, but we refuse your wedding present. We don't want it, either. That life isn't for us, and we prefer to stay out here, like you."

Levi finally let out his breath.

"I have a suggestion I think you'll like," said Charity, her voice still affected by tears. "When you can, send word back to your solicitor that you want the property held in trust for your children, should they want it."

"I like that idea," said Robert. "But, I'm going to include you and John's children and Levi's. That way, someone we know will be able to benefit from it."

Chapter 8

Later, John and Charity walked around the village, eager to see their new home. She marveled at the beadwork on shirts and moccasins and the intricate designs on baskets and wall mats. As they walked by, women looked up, giving them a quick nod before returning to their work. Naked children peeked around their mothers to watch them with round-eyed curiosity.

It was summer, and most of the women wore very little clothing—short skirts woven of natural fibers with small vests draped over their shoulders—while the children wore nothing at all.

"I don't think I have the nerve to dress like that…, which is a shame," said Charity, eyeing her husband for his response. "Since it does look cooler than the long dresses and petticoats I used to wear."

"I don't want others to see that much of your beautiful body. I like you in all of your clothes. You know how much I like it when you wear nothing at all, but that's only for me to see."

"Look, there's Levi," she said, pointing to the young people standing under the council tree. "He's talking to that girl who resembles Gray Dove. Come to think of it, I wonder if she's a younger sister. It's a good thing you taught him to speak some Cherokee language on the way here, otherwise he wouldn't be so confident now."

"That's true, he wouldn't be nearly so at ease with those young women. I wonder how much her dowry will be." John said, quietly. "Levi earned part of the goods we brought here, so I think we can manage the dowry when he needs it. He's kind of young, though, to be thinking of marriage."

"Just because he's talking to a girl doesn't mean he's ready to get married, John. I think you're jumping the gun here. He's just being a normal young man around a bunch of pretty girls. By the way, how old are you, John?"

"I guess I just turned twenty lately. It's hard to keep track of time out here."

"You mean I robbed the cradle?"

"Maybe. How old are you, since we're asking?"

"I turned twenty last spring. I was already an old maid when you married me."

"If Levi knew how it feels to have a woman like you waiting for him each day, he'd rush to get married."

"Does it help to be in love with that person?"

"You know it does. We have to get us a place of our own real quick. I can't stand being with you and not making love to you. I'll talk to Robert about getting us a lodge, or building our own, whichever is the fastest."

John looked up in time to see Robert coming out of the council hall and walked over to speak with him.

Meanwhile, Charity stood watching how Levi handled himself with his admirers. Back home he would never have developed so quickly, because at the settlement, he was considered property and always under someone's thumb.

One of the young men approached Levi with a bow and quiver. After a brief discussion, Levi left the young woman, fetched his weapon, and walked with him into the woods. The girl followed Levi with sad eyes until he disappeared and then went back to work.

Later in the day, John and Robert approached Charity who was sitting under a tree mending clothes. From their grim expressions, she knew something was up. "What is it? What's the matter?" She asked.

"We were just in the council hall for a meeting, and it appears we're caught in a war between the Cherokee and the Shawnee. One faction wants to go to war, and another group wants to move farther west to get away from it all. Besides that, we can't go back now, even if we wanted to—there are too many Indians lusting for war all over the mountains."

In view of the peaceful scene in front of her, it was hard to imagine it could all go up in smoke. "That leaves us in the middle, right? Is there danger to this village?"

"We don't know the answer for sure." John answered. "Scouts have gone out to see how close the danger is. Where's Levi?"

"He left with some young braves about an hour ago," she replied.

"Did he say where they were going?"

"No, but I don't think they went hunting deer. I'm afraid he's with the group sent to see how close the danger is."

"Robert says there's a lodge we can move into. Want to go look at it?" From the look in his eyes, Charity knew he had more on his mind than a place to live.

"Why do some of the people want to move?" she asked, but he stopped her in mid-sentence, saying, "I'll tell you when we get alone"

As they walked to the lodge, curiosity got the better of her. "We're alone now John, so tell me, why do some of the people want to move and leave all this behind?" She looked out over the vast ripening fields before entering the lodge.

"Honey, do you know that the Cherokee have no set rules against adultery? The young can have relations with others before they marry, and some of the women have other men, even after taking a husband."

"No, I didn't know that. What does that have to do with moving the entire village? I've never seen such good crops, acres and acres of beans and squash growing among the maize. Look at all that. It's beautiful, and it's such a lush valley. I hear they get two crops a year. It just doesn't make sense to me."

"Ahhh, he dropped his head before continuing. "Did you know they consider a man's seed a pollutant? Anything touched by it has to be cleaned, and they have ceremonies just for that. They bathe and wash anything touched by it, bodies, clothes, mats, and such."

"John, you're beating around the bush. Why don't you just tell me what you're getting at?"

"From what Robert told me, some of the young married people have been swapping wives, and they did it in the fields at night. According to the elders, they've pushed down poles holding bean vines, trampling maize and squash as they romped and enjoyed their pleasures with each other. They've polluted the fields with lust, and it's a big job to have the ceremonies to cleanse hundreds of acres. The guilty aren't even sorry for the trouble they caused, and they continue to play in the crops at night. People hear them chasing each other, squealing and laughing in the fields. When the elders try to catch them, the young slink away and mock them. It's a bad omen for the village. They consider harmony essential to Cherokee life. These kinds of actions breed disharmony."

"I would think it breeds wives, too. Not necessarily your wife, either," Charity said as she tried to imagine running naked through fields on hot summer nights, being chased by an ardent lover. If the lover was John, she would be easy to catch, she considered and blushed.

"Did you just imagine you chasing me through the fields? Or was I chasing you up and down the maize rows? What would we do when we caught each other?"

"You know what we'd do."

"Would it be something like this?" He pulled her to him and started an exploration of her body as he kissed her.

"No, it would be more like this." Reaching down, she caught the bottom of his shirt and pulled it off him. She planted kisses across his chest as she pulled the strings holding his pants.

"Oh, the fields wouldn't be safe from us, either, if we were out there," he said as her shirt and pants slid to the floor. Their bodies soon followed the clothes as pent up passion took control.

***

After being in the village for several days, they walked out to see fields of maize, beans, and squash stretching as far as the eye could see. In the distance, a flock of crows prepared to land, but a screech scattered them flapping into the air. When the birds tried to land again, yet another scream sent them into a panic as they tried to gain altitude.

Spooked herself, Charity asked John, "What was that?"

"See those little huts dotting both sides of the fields? They are for the *watchers*. Women who are too old to work the fields sit there during the day and do bead work, work on skins, anything they like, but when the crows fly in, the women screech, and it scares the crows away."

"Those women do a better job than stuffed scarecrows," Charity responded with a laugh. "At home, birds like scarecrows. First they eat their fill, rest on the scarecrow, burp a few times, and then empty their bowels on its head before going back for more.

Laughing, John held her close by his side as they walked back to the village together. When his fingers strayed to caress her breast, Charity gasped.

Aroused by his touch, she whispered, "You know what that does to me."

"Yep, I sure do," he replied with a wicked grin.

They approached the village, and Robert called out to John. "The elders are meeting in the council house to decide where to move if war comes this way. They asked if you would sit with us."

John groaned and kissed her before pulling away to join Robert. Charity grinned as he turned away to reposition himself, knowing exactly what he wanted to do. Sitting in a war council it.

***

Sitting in the council hall around the ceremonial fire, John heard the history of the people and the land. For the first time in his years on the frontier, he realized how much the settlers and the Indian's governmental processes resembled one another. For both, finding the path of wisdom and leading large groups to it was a challenge.

One of the speakers was particularly eloquent. "This is our home, and our ancestors are buried here. Our crops are almost ready to harvest for winter. And if we move, where would we go, north closer to the Shawnee? Or south near the Creeks? If we head towards the east, it will bring us even closer to the whites that already crowd us. That leaves only the mountains to the west."

John was sitting with Robert, pondering what he had just heard when a group of well-traveled warriors, Levi among them, entered the hall.

The group leader addressed the war chief with grave respect, giving report on their findings. The elder stared at them as though memorizing each face before speaking to the assembly.

"These young men have just returned from scouting the war zone. They've seen Cherokee villages laid waste, crops burned, the people enslaved. The war is coming toward us. What is more important, saving our people, or dying where our ancestors lie? I propose we send out parties to the west, over the mountains, to find a new home for this village. Those who remain can harvest the crops and prepare for the long journey."

John was leaving the meeting when Robert stopped him.

"I've been asked to lead one of the scouting parties for a new home for the village. I think Gray Dove's father suggested it. This may be his way of getting rid of me by sending me over the mountains," He chuckled. "But, I'm going to fool the old goat by taking Gray Dove with me. Will you go with us?"

"I will go, but I won't leave Charity behind. Knowing her, she wouldn't let me leave without her if I tried. As you know, she can be pretty stubborn."

"Tell her I am taking Gray Dove with me. The old man thinks I might not come back, and Gray Dove would be free to marry again. That's not the only reason—she'll know what to look for out there. If we find a good place, we could stay there and send word back. So yes, since she already knows the hardships of trail life, bring Charity with you. What do you say?"

"Let me discuss this with Charity. If she doesn't want to go, neither will I."

John returned to find Charity sitting just outside the lodge, waiting for him. She watched as he approached and said in a soft voice, "That must have been some meeting. You were gone for hours."

The moon was rising in the night sky, the same full moon as on the night they wed. John took Charity's hand and pulled her to her feet, saying, "This must be our three month anniversary. Shouldn't we celebrate?"

"I figured you'd want to start where we left off," she replied with a grin. She held his arm close as they walked to the fields where maize tassels waved gently in the night air.

"We aren't going to pollute the maize fields tonight, are we? You know how much trouble that causes."

"Tonight is our anniversary, and we're going somewhere special," he said, approaching one of the stilted huts. "See the moon is full, just barely peeking over the mountains, just like the night we said our vows. Now, climb up this ladder."

"Ohhh, I see how your mind works. We're going to celebrate our anniversary high above the fields. At least we won't pollute the crops that way."

John followed her up the ladder, his face so close it was level with her enticing buttocks. With a groan he nipped her gently on one cheek. Startled, she laughed and darted up the ladder with him close behind. They forgot to welcome the moon as it bathed the land with soft light. Instead, they celebrated their love for one another. They were so intent on their own pleasure, they missed the squeals and laughter coming from the fields below.

When the faintest hint of dawn streaked the morning sky, John woke Charity, kissing her lips, her eyes, her cheeks, and then back to her lips.

"Good morning, sleepyhead. Wake up, there's something we need to discuss."

"Ummm, I like the way you wake me." Her eyes barely open, she sat up. "What do we need to discuss? Is it how we are going to get back before anyone sees us up here? Or are we going to stay and shock the watcher when she climbs up?"

"Come on, we need to get out of here before she comes."

"So, I guess we aren't going to shock anyone this morning?"

"Maybe next time, but not today." He kissed her shoulder as she pulled her pants on. You're much too tempting for me to ever let you out of my sight."

"All right," she pulled her shirt over her head. "Now I'm dressed. Let's go have that discussion. It had better be worth it if I have to miss morning lovemaking.

They left the hut just before the first of the watchers arrived.

At the Council Tree he told her, "The council has asked Robert and me to take one of the scouting parties across the mountains to find a suitable location for the village. I don't want to leave you here without friends or family, and I won't go if you don't want me to. The alternative is for you to go with us. The journey here was hard, but I think this one will be even more so. Would you want to make the trip? If not, we'll stay here together until the village moves."

"Would there be time alone for love in the moonlight?"

"There had better be, or I'm not going."

"But, you think the trip will be as difficult, or maybe harder, than the one coming here?"

"Yes, harder and more dangerous."

Charity observed his expression as he waited for her answer. *He expects me to say I won't attempt such a journey again*, she thought.

"John, you were made for this life. You revel in the challenge, the constant danger, and the thrill of beating the odds. Me, on the other hand, I like soft beds and a full stomach."

Cut to the quick, he bowed his head at her words and missed her smile. When she saw his response, she tipped his head back up with both hands and kissed him deeply.

"Go get our packs ready, John. Of course, I'll go with you. While it's true I do love a soft bed and a full stomach, I would expect you'll make sure I get them when we find our new home."

"You incredible woman, I'm glad I was smart enough to marry you. I promise to provide you with a full stomach as often as possible. As far as the soft bed goes, I promise to find you such a bed. I like the idea of you lying on it, waiting for me."

Making haste, they readied their packs for the long journey over the western mountains. They carried everything they had, including trade items, on their backs, leaving nothing to chance.

They were waiting for Robert and Gray Dove to join them when Levi ran up with his pack. "You can't go without me." He cast a hurt look at Charity and then added, "You would leave your own brother behind?"

"Don't look at me, I had nothing to do with this," said Charity. "I just found out this morning and have been working ever since." Somewhat mollified, Levi turned to help her with her pack when she added, "Are you sure you want to go? You seem to have a lot of admirers here, and it appears you've been in the maize with one of them. You were with one particular girl most of the time," Charity said, pulling a maize husk off his collar, "the one who favors Gray Dove."

***

Levi realized his clothes were in disarray, and his hair was full of maize tassels. Blushing, he brushed himself off, saying with a grin, "I'll have to admit the attention has been flattering, but I can't let you go without me—you and John are my family." He was still for a moment, before continuing.

"She's Gray Dove's younger sister. I really, really like her, no, I love her, but when I asked for her hand, her father refused me. The old man frowned every time he saw me near her, but she said she'd wait for me anyway."

Robert watched the other two scouting parties leave the camp, then he slapped Levi on the back, telling him, "Good to have you, Levi. I'm glad to have another dependable man along with us. Would you take point? John will take the middle to protect the women, and I'll bring up the rear."

They headed west, away from the lush fields and the safety of the village and into the woods. They had gone less than a mile when Levi held up his arm and stopped.

"I saw movement over there," he pointed to a thick clump of elderberry bushes. "There's at least one person in there, maybe more."

Staying with the packs, Gray Dove pulled her knife and Charity notched an arrow in readiness. The men circled the elderberries as Levi silently approached the place where he'd seen movement. With a blood-curdling yell, he charged into the clump of bushes and tall grass with his tomahawk ready. What happened next was truly comic.

The men could see that Levi was struggling with his victim, but there was something odd about it. Fully expecting to see Indians attack from the woods, they stood ready to fight until Levi sat up rather quickly. Obviously bewildered, he stayed where he was without getting up, only his head visible in the tall grass.

When he failed to speak, John asked, "Levi, what's wrong?"

With a sheepish look on his face, Levi finally answered. "I'm fine. I just can't get up."

When the women joined them, they all moved closer to where Levi sat in the grass. Pinned beneath him was a young woman they all knew.

"Levi, let that girl up. She can't breathe."

"I can't."

"Why not?"

"It's Singing Girl, and she's furious with me." He turned his neck to show them several, long bleeding scratches. "If I let her up, she'll attack me again."

"I can see that, but why is she so furious with you?" Gray Dove asked.

When Levi let up just enough to allow the girl a lungful of air, she burst out with, "I love him, and I am angry with him. When I asked him to take me with him, he refused. Now, he is leaving me behind, because Father is asking a huge dowry for me, just as he did you, Sister. When Levi asked Father for my hand, he was refused. Levi doesn't have the dowry so he is going away and leaving me behind." With that, she broke into sobs, and Levi took her in his arms.

Shocked, Levi held her, "I told you, I'd get the dowry. Didn't you believe me?"

"I believed you, but Father promised me to another as soon as he saw you leave. I ran and ran to catch you," she cried, her voice muffled against his shirt.

Gray Dove spoke. "Our father is very stubborn. If Robert had left me in the village and gone back east with John, Father would have married me to another as soon as he left. Robert was wise to stay, or he would have lost me."

"I see the resemblance between the two of you," said Charity. "You are both so attractive that I don't blame men for falling in love with either of you, so I'm sure your father knew he could get high marriage dowries."

Before Levi could say anything, John spoke. "Do you want to marry Singing Girl? If so, we're still close enough to the village to go back. You can use your share of the trade goods to pay the dowry, and then she can come with us."

"John, is this true? You would do that for me?"

John replied with a grin, "I guess that means you want her. Families have to stick together, so let's go back and pay the old man his pound of flesh."

"Oh, no. He does not want flesh," Singing Girl piped up. "He wants more of your arrowheads, beads, and some of that bright ribbon."

They made quite a sensation on their return to the village. The entire community turned out to see what was happening, and soon, all were aware of the old man's duplicity. There was little he could do when Levi presented him with the bride price but accept it while looking sheepish. Singing Girl, however, still had concerns. "Levi, even though Father accepted the dowry, it will take two weeks to prepare for the wedding, and you need to be on the trail. Will you still take me with you?"

Surprised by the question, Levi responded by taking her in his arms and saying, "What do you think?" to laughter all around.

It took very little time for Charity to see Levi and Singing Girl were under considerable strain. With the bride price paid, a major barrier keeping them apart was down. Now they were traveling in close proximity every minute of the day, and sexual tensions were building.

Gray Dove, protective of her sister, tried to keep her close, but Singing Girl didn't want protection. She wanted Levi.

John and Charity walked away from the camp to find some privacy in the cool night air. When John's hand crept up from her waist to her breasts, Charity stopped him.

"Before we let pleasure distract us, let's talk about Levi and Singing Girl."

Irritated, he pulled back. "What about them?"

"Desire is driving them crazy and I remember what that was like. Levi won't make love to her until they are married, and she's making it very difficult for him to resist."

Drawing her close, he nuzzled her neck, sending waves of desire through her entire body. He whispered in her ear. "Does it matter this minute? I'm more interested in you."

She held out for only a moment, trying to concentrate on Levi and Singing Girl. She failed.

The next morning, when John and Robert walked out to answer the call of nature, Robert told him. "You have to do something about Levi and Singing Girl."

"What do you mean, I have to do something? She's your wife's sister."

Levi is your wife's brother." Robert retorted.

"Oh, all right. What is it I have to do?"

"Get them together. We can't slip into the woods like you and Charity, because Singing Girl keeps us awake half the night, talking to Gray Dove and looking over at Levi. It will be a miserable trip for us if we can't fix this."

Before he could say anything more, Robert spotted bear tracks in front of them. "Uh oh…."

"What?"

"Bear. A big one by the look of those tracks, and they are fresh. From the way it drags one leg it's injured. That makes it more dangerous, especially if it can't hunt. Let's get back to camp."

Back in camp, John called the group together to discuss the tracks Robert had found. "The danger is minimal if we stay together since they don't usually attack groups. Keep your weapons at hand, and nobody is to wander off alone. Levi, I'll take point today."

Leaving Robert to help the women break camp, John signaled Levi to follow him back to the tracks.

"Wow, that's a big one." Levi said with a frown, "Just look at the size of those paws." They tracked the bear down to the stream, lost the trail, and returned to camp. On the way back, John started to ask Levi about Singing Girl, but Levi got there first.

"Since we're away from the women, can I talk to you about something?"

"Of course, what is it?"

"You know I love Singing Girl. She's all I think of. I'm afraid I'm not much good to anyone right now with wanting her so much.

That's the second time I've heard that complaint today, John thought as Levi continued.

"What does this have to do with me?"

"We don't want to wait any longer. Will you help us marry, like I helped you and Charity?"

"What? I can't—" John said, and stopped himself mid-sentence. You need…, you need…, Oh, I see your point. You took part in the pledging ceremony for Charity and me, didn't you?"

"Exactly," said the young man. "You pledged to one another out there on the trail, and you are happy together. I've watched. I want Singing Girl and me to have that same opportunity."

"It's not the kind of ceremony or the place that makes a marriage special, Levi. It's about how two people feel about each other. Look at Robert and Gray Dove. They had a traditional Indian ceremony and they're happy, too."

"So, you'll help us marry?"

"How can I refuse? Do you want everyone there?"

"Oh, yes. We want the whole camp. It's the right thing to do, and the right time to do it," Levi said as they walked back to camp.

On their return, John and Levi told the others more about the bear signs. "Its spore was fresh, but we lost the trail in the creek. I think we'll be all right as long as we stay together as much as possible. When you have to relieve yourselves, go together and one of you stand guard with your weapons. Above all, don't straggle behind. Bears don't much like groups; they like to catch careless individuals."

While John had their attention, he stood quietly for a moment before making an announcement. "I have the honor to announce the marriage of Levi to Singing Girl this evening, here in camp. You are all invited."

"John, is this for real?" Robert asked, looking at Gray Dove to see her reaction. She frowned for a moment, before breaking into a smile of joy, hugging an ecstatic Singing Girl.

"Yes, Levi asked if I'd perform a ceremony for them, today, so if you will, let's clean up the camp, get everything ready, and find a place for them to sleep. We'll have the ceremony this evening after supper."

"I guess we need to stay here for a few days." John continued. "I want to give Levi the same consideration he gave us."

After the camp was put in order, John asked Charity to help him set up the marriage bed. "I think they'll be safe up on that ledge above us. If you'll grab their blankets and some food, I'll get some water and his weapons."

"I don't think they'll need a fire, do you? We didn't," Charity said with a wicked grin.

"Having you in my bed kept me warm, woman. I liked having you keep me warm that way."

Charity looked around the mountainside and saw another ledge hidden by trees off to the right of the camp. "Let's give Robert and Gray Dove our campsite, you and I can take our bedrolls to that ledge over there. We want to give the newlyweds three days together, and we can use it, too. Or, are you tired of me already?"

"Darlin', I like the way you think. I'll let you know when I'm tired of you. Bring your luscious body up on that ledge, and I'll show you if I'm tired of you."

John went to the pond and killed a fine, fat beaver and took it to camp for the wedding supper. The smell of roasted meat was heavenly as the women made fry bread and dried fruit patties by the fire.

At supper, Levi and Singing Girl, too excited to eat, sat close together, waiting for nightfall.

That evening, John stood before them, trying to appear official. "We are gathered here today, in the sight of God and these witnesses, to see these two joined together. Levi Collins, do you take Singing Girl as your wife, to love her, and protect her, until the end of your days?"

His voice barely a whisper, Levi said, "I do." His eyes were full of love as he gazed at Singing Girl.

"Singing Girl, do you take Levi Collins as your husband, to love and care for him until the end of your days?"

She nodded her head vigorously saying, "Yes, yes," took a deep breath and added, "I do."

"In the sight of God and these witnesses, I declare you pledged together. You may kiss the bride." Before the words could leave John's mouth, Levi was ahead of him, lifting Singing Girl clean off the ground to smother her with kisses. The others clustered around them to offer good wishes until Gray Dove took Singing Girl into her arms and held her for a long time.

"Don't cry for me, Sister," Singing Girl said. Be happy I have the man I love. Just imagine what might have happened. Father was going to marry me to old Panther Claw. Ugh, I'd have been the old man's third wife."

After supper, John yawned, and grinning at Robert said, "Don't you think it's time to turn in? I'm really tired, how about you Robert?"

Robert stretched his arms and stood, saying, "Yep, I believe it's my bedtime. How about you, Gray Dove?"

When Levi stood to fetch their bedrolls he said, "Where are our bedrolls? They were right here earlier today."

"What bedrolls?" John replied. Levi failed to notice the gleam in John's eyes or to see Robert's mischievous grin. John asked, "Did you have bedrolls? I wonder where they could be."

Charity, who saw the humor, but didn't want it to get out of hand, took pity on the newlyweds. "Remember, this is not a chivaree, folks." Turning to Levi and Singing Girl, she said, "John and I returned the favor you did for us, Levi. Look up on that ledge, your bed is made. We placed your weapons, food, and water nearby. Go enjoy your honeymoon. We'll see you in three days. Now go on, before these men get any bright ideas.

From below, they heard happy laughter when the couple reached the ledge. Levi and Singing Girl leaned over the edge to call down a thank you before disappearing into the gathering darkness.

"Charity and I are going up on that ledge over there, the one with the bushes all around it," John told Robert and Gray Dove. "That leaves this camp for the two of you. How about it?"

***

Robert and Gray Dove nodded and watched them leave with relief. They could finally make love. Standing close behind her, Robert slid his arms around his wife, cupping her full breasts in his hands in the firelight.

"Come to bed with me, Gray Dove," he whispered in her ear.

In response, she turned to him and kissed him hungrily. He lifted her up and took her to their blankets.

"This reminds me of our wedding night," he said, laying her down gently.

"Why?"

"Because of my desire for you."

"Oh, Robert!"

***

John pulled Charity up the last few feet to the ledge. She said, "I hope they're as happy together as we are."

"Are you happy?"

"I'm almost happy."

"What will it take to make you a happy woman?"

"You. That and what you do with your hands and that wonderful body of yours."

"In that case, you're going to be a very, very, happy woman tonight, and tomorrow."

"What about the last day?"

"Then, you're going to be ecstatic."

Chapter 9

Dawn on the fourth day brought Levi and Singing Girl back to camp. Giggling, they slipped and slid down the bank, holding on to bedding and supplies. They stood close and touched each other often when they thought others weren't aware. Levi showed no embarrassment when kissing Singing Girl if she was close to him. They embraced and seemed to glow from happiness.

As they were breaking camp, Charity pulled Gray Dove aside to ask for some personal advice. "What do you use for your monthly time?" she asked. "When I was on the trail with John and Levi, since I was passing as a boy, I had to hide my monthly period. That time, I used cattail down rolled in a cloth. Do you know of something better?"

"Cattail down is good when you have nothing else," Gray Dove responded, "but there are better choices. Women gather a certain moss and use it the same way you did the down. It needs to be smoked to kill tiny insects living inside. Having our moon time is irritating enough when we travel without being bitten, too. The moss holds the life blood better, and we carry a supply with us always."

"Where can I find some of that moss?" I need it now."

"I always keep some in my pack, and now that I am with child I don't need it," Gray Dove told her. "Wait here and I'll bring some to you. Then I'll teach you which moss to gather and how to smoke it."

When Gray Dove returned with the smoky gray moss and a soft rabbit skin, she showed Charity how to make a pouch for the moss.

When she put it on and dressed, Charity hugged Gray Dove saying, "Oh thank you, this is much better than what I had before."

"In the village, the women have a special lodge for our moon time," Gray Dove told her. "Others bring us food and drink while we are there, and we come out only after we have ended our flow. Then the women bring us water to cleanse ourselves before we bathe in the pond. To enter the pond after our moon time without cleansing ourselves would pollute the water, and that is forbidden."

"Why do women have to be isolated during their moon time?"

"Women are impure during their moon time. If we handle our men's weapons they will not work right afterwards."

"I handled John's rifle and bow many times during my monthly time, and it didn't seem to bother his aim."

Raising an eyebrow, Gray Dove countered with, "It is also said to weaken the man if you touch him during your time."

"Now, that I know isn't true! I touched and was touched by John during my time. I didn't notice any weakening in his love making or his desire for me afterwards."

"Never tell a man this, but my mother thinks the real reason for the five days in the cabin was to give women a rest. I personally think it's to keep women from being attacked while gathering maize or picking berries far from the village, as bears are attracted to the smell of fresh blood."

Charity gave her a hug and they joined the group. John gave them a questioning look for being gone so long but said nothing.

***

The day grew hot as they made their way into the mountains. When John kept looking behind and finally called a halt, Robert asked, "What is it, John? I don't see or hear anything."

"I don't know for sure yet, but I think we're being followed."

Levi, standing behind the group, heard it first. "I can hear something shuffling behind us."

"Is that what I think it is?" Charity asked.

"If you think it's a bear, you'd be right."

"I thought you said they don't attack groups."

"I said they usually don't attack groups. This one could be hurt and not able to hunt normally. We probably can't outrun it, so we'll have to outwit it."

"How do we do that?"

"I don't know, yet. Let's just hope he goes on his way soon. The only reason why one would follow six people is the smell of blood—they can smell it for miles."

Charity turned white and took her husband's hand. "John, we have to talk, now." She said, pulling him aside.

"What is it, honey? We have to stay together; we're in danger here by ourselves."

"I'm in danger anywhere. I just started my monthly time. That bear is following me, and now I know why that other bear followed us. That was during my monthly time, too. John, what are we going to do?"

John froze as her words sunk in, his eyes so wide the whites showed all around.

"We have to think of something quick," he told their friends. "That bear is after Charity."

"What do you mean? How can you know that? Puzzled, Robert looked at them both.

John, embarrassed, tripped over his words. "Be…, because, she's a woman."

Gray Dove and Singing Girl whispered to their husbands who turned red and looked down.

"What can we do? A smart varmint like that might wait until we camp and charge during the night. Even if we stood guard, a hungry bear could swat the guard like a fly and drag Charity away." Levi shuddered, putting his arms around Singing Girl and pulling her close.

Staying close together, they discussed different methods for disposing of the bear. Charity said, "Can't we trap the bear, using me for bait? After all, I'm the one it's after."

"No!" John exploded. "The last time we used you for bait, it nearly got you killed. I won't let you go through that again."

"John, wouldn't you rather stop this right now? Otherwise, we'll be looking over our shoulders the whole journey. The bear might get in front of us and surprise us or attack at night. Sooner or later, we might let our guard down, and he will be waiting. We may not be as lucky as we were last time. I could climb a tree and wait. When the bear finds me, you all can shoot it."

"You know bears can climb trees, Charity," Robert said, speaking quietly.

"Yes, I know they can. That's why I'm counting on all of you to be good shots."

"I can't risk losing you," John said. "It's too dangerous." He buried his head on her shoulder.

"John, darling, look at me, I trust you. I trust all of you. I know you won't let me down. I want to get this over with, while I still have the nerve. Now, let's find a suitable tree with open ground under it. I want all of you to have a good field of vision."

When they found a large walnut tree standing alone in the open, Charity shimmied up the trunk and settled in to wait.

The bear approached slowly, breathing heavily as it limped along behind them, staying on their trail. The men positioned themselves in a semi-circle behind some trees, the rifles, powder, and shot at the ready.

John loaded his rifle, sliding the ramrod down on the wadding and packed the ball in. This shot had to count, as he would have to reload after each shot. His bow and his quiver filled with arrows laid beside him.

Nerves stretched thin as the black bear, sniffing the air, lifted his massive head. Knowing its prey had stopped, it sampled the air, nostrils distended, scenting fear. The delicious aroma of blood made the bear's stomach rumble, propelling it to the source.

Charity, frozen in place, watched as the bear, dragging its injured hind leg behind, shuffled into the clearing. Sighting prey, the bear charged, catching them all off guard. Lunging, its sharp, curved claws sank deep into the tree's thick bark as it began to climb.

The men aimed and fired as one, reloaded and shot again. But the bear, pumped with adrenalin, failed to notice the lead balls tearing into his body. Ignoring them and the injured leg hampering its progress, the desperate bear clawed its way up the tree.

Charity inched further out on the tree limb as the bear approached. She was twenty feet up the tree, too high to jump.

John, frantic now, reloaded for a third shot but the bear, undeterred, shivered slightly, and continued to climb. Notching an arrow in his bow, John aimed at the spot behind the bear's forearm for a heart shot. His arrow sank in deep, tearing into the thick hide, but the bear kept climbing.

The bear, now less than six feet away from Charity's fragile perch, shook the entire tree with its weight. With her bow, Charity could have shot straight into its gaping mouth, but the bow was down below. Meanwhile, the bear, finally growing weaker, paused more often.

By this time, the huge bear was loaded with multiple lead balls and arrows sticking out of its body. Gray Dove, using John's bow, and Singing Girl with Charity's bow, joined the men, sending arrow after arrow into the bear.

John watched in horror as the bear lunged ever closer to Charity. Without her, his future was cold and bleak and his life meant nothing. With a savage look on his face, John threw his weapons on the ground and raced toward the bear.

"John, no. He'll kill you. Please, John. No!" Charity screamed, watching him race toward the tree.

The bear took no notice of John when he took a running leap to grab the lowest limb and scrambled up limb by limb until he could dig his hands into thick fur. Now with firm handholds, John wrapped his legs around the huge body. Holding tight with his left hand he pulled his knife and slashed at the bear's throat, drew back and slashed repeatedly, driven by his fear for Charity's life.

Bear blood spurted under his hands, splattering the tree, and gushing over his knife. The bear, maintaining its hold on the tree, twisted around, trying to sink sharp fangs in his hand. John held on with a death grip, slashing and twisting the blade into the massive throat. Only when the jugular vein severed did the bear's strength falter.

John jumped off and rolled away as the bear crashed to the ground, legs kicking, jaws still snapping at the air.

When Charity saw John's blood-splattered body lying prone on the ground beneath her, she appeared to be horrified. Half sliding, half jumping, she scrambled down the tree. Avoiding the still-twitching bear, she raced to her husband's side.

When she reached him, he lay face down in the beaten grass, covered with blood. Still watching the twitching bear, she covered John's body with her own. When she was positive he was alive, beginning with a minute examination of his face, she searched for claw marks. She frantically ran her hands over his body, leaving bloody trails everywhere she touched.

When he tried to speak, she lowered her ear to his mouth for what might be his last words.

"I love your hands all over me. But can you wait until tonight?"

His wife jumped back as if a snake had bitten her, then fell on top of him crying, "Oh, John, I was so scared. Are you hurt anywhere?"

"Just one place."

"Where?"

"Where you have my face pushed into the ground."

The others arrived just in time to see Charity slap her husband playfully on the head. She turned to them and said, "He isn't hurt, but I may finish what the bear started if he ever scares me like that again."

"Do you want to compare scared?" John asked, sitting up to wipe his bloody hands on the grass. "How about seeing your wife up a tree, posing as bait, and a hungry bear with dinner on his mind after her. Your bullets and arrows barely faze him. That goes beyond scared, that's sheer terror. Don't ever put me through that again."

As their adrenalin levels dropped, exhaustion set in. John stared at the dead bear and the blood covered ground before saying, "We'll take all the fresh meat we can carry. We need the fat for energy, and his meat will keep us going better than venison. Let's butcher him right now and get out of here before the fresh blood lures others. I want to be far away when other bears and cougars smell blood."

It took most of the afternoon to skin the bear and cut the meat. By the time they were done, each member of the party had twenty extra pounds to carry, all wrapped up in neat bundles of bear hide.

"We have about all we can carry, but let's find a campsite soon near a stream and get you cleaned up. We don't want another bear following us," Robert said.

While John took the soap root to a nearby stream to clean up, Gray Dove and Singing Girl set to work gathering vines. They stripped off the outer bark and braided the inner strips into ropes. They suspended the raw meat high in a tree to keep it away from predators.

The next morning, they cut the meat into strips and dried it by the fire. "We might as well take time to dry it properly," John said, grinning at his wife. "We need the food, and I don't want Charity's efforts to go to waste."

"You better savor every piece," she shot back at him. "I'm not sitting up in a tree again to entice a hungry bear."

"I don't know if I could have sat up in a tree while a bear came looking for me," Levi said, shaking his head. "And I know I couldn't have let Singing Girl do it." Turning to Charity, he added, "You sure had a lot more faith in us than I did."

"Little brother, we had no choice. It was either that or have the bear charge through camp one night, killing everyone in its path just to drag me away."

"With all this meat, we won't have to hunt and we can travel faster." Robert said. "Gray Dove has heard stories of this area. She thinks we may find a suitable valley soon, and if so, we can send word back to the village."

"Yes, the villagers will be anxious to get settled and plant a second crop of the season." Gray Dove added. "Without that crop we may face another starving time next spring."

Chapter 10

Two days later, the travelers found what appeared to be an abandoned village nestled in a lush valley. With no watchers to chase them away, crows feasted on ripening maize.

"Something's wrong here," John whispered in the stillness. "This village appears to have been deserted."

Robert agreed, indicating either warfare or disease could have wiped them out.

Entering the village, their weapons at the ready, they saw weeds growing between some lodges, something no healthy village allowed. Skinny dogs hid behind houses, barking. It was an eerie place, appearing to be empty, and yet they felt eyes watching their approach.

As the party entered—right hands up in the sign of peace—one face peered around a buffalo hide flap. The old man stepped into the plaza, clearly wary of the strangers. He raised his arm toward them.

"He's Yuchi." Gray Dove says, "It has been years since we've traded with them. As I know some of their tongue, I will speak with him." Using sign language and her knowledge of Yuchi, she spoke with the elder at length. With a differential nod of her head, she returned to the others saying, "According to the ancient one, this village was strong until disease nearly wiped them out last year. Since then they've struggled to survive. Two weeks ago a trader came and stayed many days. He had trade goods not seen before, like French hair brushes and mirrors, which he traded for sexual favors from the women. He traded knives and hatchets to the men. He was an artist and drew pictures of the people standing in front of their lodges with their new possessions. He left one day, returning the next with twenty Iroquois warriors, the first ever seen this far south. Catching them by surprise, the warriors gathered up the young people, both men and women. They left the very old and the very young. Using his drawings, the trader located all the goods he had traded and stripped the houses of everything of value. He said he'd sell them at the next village.

"The Iroquois wanted to massacre the rest, but he laughed saying they would provide a new crop of slaves in the future. Now, they're too weak to defend themselves, and they fear all newcomers."

"Tell them we mean them no harm, and we are looking for a new place to settle our people," Robert said, watching the elder's face. "And ask his permission to camp here."

Gray Dove did as he asked, then listened carefully to the answer. When she turned back to her husband, she said, "He says we can camp here. Since we are stronger than them, how can he refuse?"

"Ask him what language the trader spoke. Did he speak English or French?"

"He says the trader spoke French and you are the first English he's ever seen."

"Tell him we're here in peace, and we're moving our village due to the big wars over the mountains. Does he know of a suitable valley where we might settle and plant our crops?"

The conversation was long. The elder pointed up and down the valley as they spoke, gesturing first toward himself and then at them.

"I can't tell if he's telling us to leave their valley, or what." Levi watched the conversation with interest.

Gray Dove turned to them, her face serious. Charity's heart dropped, thinking, he wants us to go away.

Gray Dove said, "This is Big Bear, once Peace Chief of this village. He says the valley is long and will hold many people, and there are only a few of his people left. If we treat the Yuchi with respect and not as conquered people, we can make this our home. These lodges are empty, and the crops are already planted. His only request is that we provide safeguard to the old women, so they can scare away the crows and save the maize."

"I said we would discuss his proposal," she told the group. "The Cherokee and the Yuchi have always been friends. Let it stay so."

Robert grinned at her. "You said it better than we could have." He turned to Big Bear and raised his hand in peace.

***

The travelers agreed to join the Yuchi, and stay in the valley. When Gray Dove related their decision to Big Bear, his aged face broke into a toothless grin. When he called his people to come into the plaza, they were shocked to see Big Town held only a few dozen people—the very young and the very old.

Seeing their surprise, Big Bear said, "In our father's time, we had a sickness come to our village. It killed many and we had just recovered enough to defend ourselves. The Shawnee could have killed us all, but they had the sickness at the same time. Between the latest sickness and now the kidnappings, you see our numbers are greatly reduced. It will be good to help this village recover. Meanwhile many houses await new occupants. Find yours and settle in."

John and Charity found an empty house and went inside. Reed rugs covered hard-packed dirt floors and brightly colored mats lined the walls, just like in the Cherokee lodges. Charity sighed when she saw the bed with its woven blankets and rich layers of fur.

John heard her sigh and took her in his arms saying, "What is it? Why did you sigh just now? Is it because you're alone with me and know I'm going to make love to you?"

"Of course it is. Now, I have you and that soft bed you promised me."

The next morning when Robert and John went out with the old women to check the maize, they were startled to see warriors in the distance. Hurrying the women in front of them, they went back to the village to sound the alarm.

When the men arrived in the village, they were ready, but when Big Bear saw the warriors, he told them to stand down. To their surprise, he embraced one and had a water gourd brought to them.

"This is my grandson, Quick Elk, and these men are from this village," he told them. "They've escaped the slavers and returned to us. Let them catch their breath and we'll hear their story."

"The slavers ran us many miles the first day." Quick Elk told them. "They were happy to have caught so many Yuchi with no losses of their own, and the Frenchman was very satisfied with our capture. He goaded the women who had pleasured him for his trade goods, telling them they were easy to capture, and all it took was a few trinkets."

"How did you manage to get away?" John asked.

"The Frenchman made us carry his plunder, and the packs had knives in them. We took one of the knives to cut our bonds and slipped away late last night. We ran until we fell, rested, and ran some more. We hoped there would be enough warriors to help us release the rest of our people. But I can see there are not."

"We're here," Robert declared for his group who nodded in agreement.

Big Bear's grandson stared at the white man long and hard before answering. "You are white like the trader who killed and kidnapped our people. Why should we trust you?"

"Slavers are our enemies, too," Robert told him. "If those Iroquois slavers get away with raiding this far south, no village will be safe. We live with a band of Eastern Cherokee who want to move here and live in safety and peace with the Yuchi. To make this valley safe again, we are willing to join with you to defeat the Frenchman and his friends."

Big Bear called his people into the council house to discuss Robert's proposal. While they waited, Robert turned back to his friends and said, "I spoke for all of us just now, but if you choose not to fight, stay back and help those who must remain behind. I will fight with them if they'll have me."

Robert turned to Gray Dove, whose slender body barely showed her pregnancy. "I must go, but I wish you to stay here."

She shook her head and slipped her hand under his arm saying, "We have a debt to pay to these people, my husband. If not, we'll be no better than the Frenchman and his Iroquois followers. Moreover, we three women can all use a bow."

John looked over at Charity, and she and Singing Girl were both nodding in agreement.

Big Bear formally accepted their help when he and the warriors rejoined them. Before they left, Big Bear gave Quick Elk his sling.

"Take this with you, grandson. You were always good with it; it is as silent as you need to be."

Quick Elk easily found the trail left by the kidnappers by retracing his own. "It took us two days of running from the north to reach home. As I've hunted this country many times, I think I know where they'll camp in the coming days."

"Good," John said with a grim smile. "If we hurry, maybe we can get ahead of them and make life miserable for those renegades. What is the country like up there? Are there any steep hills or canyons we could use?"

"Yes, there's one narrow pass through those hills. But if we ambush them, they'll just hide behind our people and get them killed."

"I don't want to just reach them. I want to get past them," John reminded Quick Elk. "Tell us what you know about the Iroquois. What do they fear?"

With Quick Elk leading them, they made good time the first day. The next morning he discovered tracks indicating the Yuchi captives were dragging behind as much as possible and leaving tracks easy to trace. The following day, Quick Elk sent one of his men ahead to find the Iroquois and their captives. He found them near one of the canyons and returned late in the afternoon with the news.

Moving past the slavers in the dead of night, they positioned themselves on a ridge high above the narrow canyon. By sunup, they had stacked rocks and boulders in strategic places and waited.

From his position on the ledge, John watched the captives struggle up the pass with warriors behind them. "When the warriors are directly below us, each of you take a fist-sized rock and choose your target. On my signal, try to hit them on the head. Once they are down, we'll start a controlled avalanche to cut the captives off from their captors. We need to take out as many as possible."

He turned to Quick Elk. "I saw you practicing with your sling—if you get the chance, I hope you'll aim for the Frenchman." Without a word, Quick Elk loaded a stone, aimed, and deftly swung his sling, knocking a pinecone off a distant tree. John grinned and said, "Good shot. Do that to the Frenchman, and we'll all thank you."

Quick Elk's party lay in the hot sun on the ridge. They observed the slavers taunting the exhausted prisoners struggling up the steep incline. Heavily laden, the captives were unable to avoid the unwanted touches, pinches, and yanks of hair that made them even more miserable.

Quick Elk gave the signal for the assault to begin as the Iroquois in the lead approached. Unaware of the danger, they walked straight into an avalanche of rocks and boulders. Quick Elk, watching for the Frenchman, took aim and released the sling. Stunned by the walnut-sized rock that hit his right eye, the man fell, then recovered and scrambled for cover.

The captured Yuchi quickly ducked under an overhang as the rocks came crashing down. When the landslide was over, three Iroquois warriors lay still, but the Frenchman had made his escape.

Following the ridge, they soon outpaced the slavers, camping by a small beaver pond at nightfall. They ate in silence, ignoring the flaming setting sun that seemed to set the world on fire. They slept hard.

With storm clouds on the horizon, the group decided to use their hiding place to rest up and strategize their moves.

Thunder shook the ground with the storm's approach. John watched the roiling clouds, his eyes half-closed and deep in thought. He barely noticed when Charity joined him.

Just above them, a burned-out hickory tree leaned precariously over the edge, its stark limbs raking the sky, the base burned and scarred. Seeing the tree's fragile grip on the earth, Charity instinctively measured its length and the distance to a spot on the trail below.

John, who had learned early on of her spatial ability, stood back and watched.

Puzzled by her stance and intense concentration, Robert asked, "What is she doing?"

"She can be devious when she's like this, so don't break her concentration."

Seeing Robert's perplexed reaction, John grinned adding, "Just be quiet, we have to let her mind work. Frankly, I'm glad it's directed against the Iroquois and not at us."

The men gave Charity the time and space she required and were startled when she said, "We want the Iroquois to think nature is against them. If we time it just right, using that dead tree up there, we might be able to give those renegades a good scare."

The lone hickory, its base slowly rotting, held a tenuous grasp on the earth. Thunder rumbled as they put their shoulders to the tree, working it back and forth like a loose tooth. They kept at it until the last good root snapped.

Wiping sweat from his eyes, Levi complained, "Why didn't we just cut it? That would have been faster."

"Because, we want them to think Mother Nature did it." Charity told him. "All we need is thunder and lightning when this tree crashes on top of the Iroquois." The wind picked up as she spoke with angry boiling and roiling clouds crashing into one another."

Watching the progress of the slavers and the storm, John prayed their timing was right. The wind's velocity was fierce, pushing against the tree as the men strained to hold it in place.

Charity, watching as the renegades led their captives through the pass, gloated over the Frenchman's swollen eye. Would the Gods of thunder and lightning come to their aid?

No sooner had the thought entered her mind when a powerful streak of lightning, followed by a deafening clap of thunder, struck nearby. Jagged bolts of lightning danced all around them, until aided by the wind, the tree flew from their arms and careened down the cliff to land on top of the unsuspecting Iroquois in the lead.

The Yuchi captives, walking behind the slavers, suffered only minor whip marks and scratches from wildly slashing limbs, but their captor's losses were heavy. Dazed, they stared around in shock until Small Turtle chanced to see Quick Elk's face grinning above him. With a barely perceptible nod, he acknowledged the warrior, then ducked his head to keep others from following his gaze.

Quickly Small Turtle leaned into the man tied to him and whispered. The tale went from person to person all the way up and down the line. At Small Turtle's command, the captives stood up as though obviously terrified, women began to wail; others cowered, arms over their heads.

The wind whistled like a demon and pieces of the dead tree continued to snap like gunshot where it fell. The remaining Iroquois, their hair standing on end, wanted to run when the Yuchi began pulling at the ropes, their eyes jerking around in fear,

Unharmed, the Frenchman saw their fright as he rose from the debris. As he stepped over the dead and injured still trapped under the tree, he muttered to himself. "*Mon Dieu*! Stupid Indians. They are always frightened of something."

"What? What is it you are so scared of? I see nothing but an old rotted tree loosened by a roll of thunder and a random strike of lightning. It was an accident. You hear me? Just an accident."

Small Turtle spoke, saying, "That was no accident. No Yuchi were harmed, just Iroquois. That tree and the rockslide were the work of the spirit that roams this mountain. He only allows people with pure hearts to cross this pass. We leave him offerings to keep us safe. Those who do evil are tormented by the Mountain Spirit."

"There is no such thing as a bad spirit," yelled the Frenchman. "That's just stupid superstition. Get up all of you, and let's get off this cursed mountain."

Without realizing it, the Frenchman used the wrong word to describe the mountain, and his own men rolled their eyes and looked over their shoulders.

The idea planted, the damage done, the Iroquois kept looking back as they recovered the wounded from under the tree's debris. Counting the two killed by the tree, three dead at the rockslide, and four with broken bones, it meant there were only eleven able men to care for their own injured and to watch thirty prisoners.

Quick Elk led his triumphant group up and over ridges, searching for a site to waylay the Iroquois. Approaching a bald spot on top of a mountain, they saw a brown bear cub busily playing with a tumblebug. Seeing the mother bear farther up the slope, facing away from them, they passed by in silence.

When they were out of range, John turned back to watch the cub and the group paused with him. Charity, knowing that look, stopped and wrapping her arms around him. "John, I don't know what you're thinking, but I'm not sitting in a tree again. Forget it."

Enjoying the feel of his wife's body so close to him, he leaned into her, eyes still on the cub and replied, "See that ledge the cub is playing on, Quick Elk? How many arrows do you think it would take to knock that small rock out from under the ledge and the cub?"

"You mean to knock him down onto the path in front of them?" Quick Elk said, mentally measuring the range.

"Yes, not to hurt him, but just to make him fall a ways—far enough to make him squeal for mama."

"I see what you mean. Timed right, the cub will cry, and Mama will come charging down after her baby just as the Iroquois pass by, yes?"

"You've got it, Quick Elk," John said with a wicked gleam in his eye. "This might be our last chance to convince the Iroquois that Mother Nature is against them. After this, we might have to make a fight of it, but at least we reduced their numbers.

"My brother, Small Turtle is down there. I signaled him that we're up here. If I know him, he will come up with a way to help us. His mind works like yours, John," Quick Elk said, clapping John on the shoulder.

Hiding in the underbrush, they kept the bears in sight as they waited for the Frenchman and his renegades to climb up the pass.

The curious cub, which had yet to encounter humans and knew no fear, lay down to watch their approach. Sensing danger, but unaware it would come from above, the Frenchman and his warriors huddled next to a large, hand-shaped boulder.

At John's signal, they let loose a volley of arrows aimed at the underpinnings of the ledge. Rocks began to give way, and the cub squealed just as the Frenchman walked by down below. Caught off guard, he jumped back as if he'd been shot.

Terrified now, the Indians scrambled away from the frightened baby bear's razor-like claws. They were so focused on the cub they failed to notice its mother charging down the hill.

Nobody wants to tangle with a mama bear. The Frenchman, in the lead, saw her racing toward them, and to save himself, grabbed one of the Indians and pushed the man directly into the bear's path. Anxious to reach her baby, she knocked him aside with one swipe of her powerful paw, neatly slicing his torso from one side to the other. His spurting blood drove the bear into a frenzy as she fought to save her cub.

The Iroquois, having had more than enough disaster meted out by Mountain Spirit, abandoned the Frenchman, the plunder, the captives, and ran.

Their departure left the Frenchman alone to face the angry brown bear. In a panic, he lurched away from her, but he wasn't quick enough. When she caught him by the back of his neck in her powerful jaws, the bones snapped. Shaking him like a rag doll, she threw the man to the ground where his lifeless body, twitching slightly, lay still.

She raised up in front of the captives crouching before her and roared, opening her bloody mouth wide to display fangs dripping with gore. Satisfied they understood her warning, she herded her cub back up the hill to safety.

The Yuchi captives rose from the crouch that had protected them as their rescuers slid down the hill, whooping and yelling, to land at their feet. Seeing four white faces amid Quick Elk's company, the Yuchi, still bound together, stared first at the strangers and then at Quick Elk.

"These people live with a band of Cherokee who want to move from their valley and join us," he told them. "Without their help, we'd never have been able to free you from the Iroquois. They planned the rockslide and the fallen tree. They even made the bear cub fall beside the Frenchman."

His brother, Small Turtle, backed him up by telling them, "After I saw you the first time, I told the Iroquois that the Spirit of the Mountain was after them, and it was the cause of all their trouble."

Quick Elk and the others laughed. "So, that's why they looked so scared. That's quick thinking. Now, that you are free, we can take our new friends with us and go home. The Peace Chief believes their addition will be good for our village."

"I know all of you are anxious to get home, but first, could we ask for your help?" Charity said to the brothers Quick Elk and Small Turtle.

"Of course, you saved our lives. We now owe you."

"We have to move the people from the Cherokee village to yours. Big Bear asked us to bring the old women watchers first, because the crows are eating your maize. We were going back for them when we had to help you escape. From here, it shouldn't be that far to the Cherokee town, and it will help both tribes.

***

The addition of so many extra people strained the housing in the Cherokee village. The Cherokee accommodated the Yuchi by putting the single men in the men's house. People took in as many women as they had room for.

Robert and Gray Dove took in Levi and Singing Girl, and others shared their homes with the welcome arrivals. Charity watched as the Cherokee struggled to house the extras, and she and John gave up their house to the newcomers.

The living arrangements settled for the time being, it was time to gather the first crop of the year. By nightfall, the center of town, piled with rows of fresh-picked maize, was the site of a harvest feast. Hungry Yuchi and Cherokee sat together and feasted on fragrant maize roasted in the fire.

After supper, a number of young couples drifted down to the creek to bathe. Gray Dove and Robert, following their lead, slid into the cool water, followed by Levi and Singing Girl.

Charity stripped and joined the other women in the water, washing her hair and scrubbing her skin clean. While she was getting used to the Indians' comfort with nudity, she was glad it was a dark night. When John swam up from behind, wrapping her in his arms, she welcomed him as his hands traced her curves under the water.

She shivered when his lips wandered from the back of her neck to her cheek to her earlobe. She gasped when he took it into his mouth and sucked it, caressing it with his tongue.

"That feels wonderful," she told him, leaning back for more. "John, let's go to our own private place in the cornfields. I want more of this."

"You aren't going to make me pick more corn, are you?" he asked, kissing her bare shoulder.

She led him to the hut they used once before and said playfully, "No corn picking for you tonight, but you may be tired in the morning."

When they entered the hut, he saw Charity had been busy. The bedding was there, waiting.

"You've thought of everything."

"Yes, I have. I provided a private place for us to sleep, and I brought our bedrolls and food. Now, when I please you, scream as much as you want. It won't bother the others," she teased.

"So, I scream, do I?" he asked. "Come here woman, and I'll show you what I'm going to do now, later, and possibly all night. I may be tired in the morning, but it'll be worth it."

***

In the close air of the council house the next morning, John found it hard to keep his mind on the discussion. When his lack of sleep caught up with him, he nodded off. His dreams were sweet as Charity's arms wrapped around him...

"John," that wasn't her voice..., it was Robert nudging him awake. "I take it you and Charity found a place to stay last night," he said with a chuckle. "I don't think you got much sleep."

Ignoring the comment, John said, "What did the council decide? I nodded off before they finished."

Robert elbowed his friend in the ribs and laughed. "John, you nodded off at the beginning, not at the finish. The tribe thanked us for our help in finding a suitable village. They are pleased that they won't have to build housing when they arrive. They will need all the food we can transport, so the Cherokee are weaving extra baskets, and we are going to help construct sleds to haul the supplies. If it takes us two weeks to get there and two back like it did the last time," he continued, "the rest of the crops should be harvested by the time we return."

Gray Dove and Charity cooked supper together while the men constructed the sleds.

"I like to add squash blossoms to my stews for flavor. Robert says it increases his desire for me." Gray Dove said, eyeing her husband as he approached. Robert grinned and wrapped his arms around her, his hands caressing her swelling belly.

"I love your cooking, but I love you more, and I already love our son growing inside you." He rubbed her stomach gently, and added, "There's so much I want to teach him."

Charity, working over the pots at the fire, overheard them and thought to herself, I'm past my moon time, we will have a child, too. That means our babies will be born a few months apart. It will be nice to have our children grow up together,

Then a new thought hit her: she couldn't recall Singing Girl having to collect and smoke moss recently. Was she with child also? If so, she must not have told Levi or he would be crowing like a rooster.

John, working on a sled nearby looked up to see her smile. "What is that for?"

"I was just thinking how happy I am for Robert and Gray Dove, and how glad I am to be with you. It's much better for all of us this way."

"Well, I'm glad you feel that way," he responded. "I feel like I've become a better man because of you."

"Well, you've made changes in me, too," she said with a secret smile. *I sure hope he's ready to extend our family.*

Moving to her side, he pulled her into his arms saying, "What was that smile for?"

"Oh, I don't think bears will be chasing me for a few months, now."

"What?" John stared at her, unable to comprehend her meaning, then his expression changed from perplexed, to surprise, and then to sudden joy.

"You mean it? Us? Yahoo!" He picked Charity up and swirled her around.

About the Author

Wanda Parker was born a history lover with strong ties to her Scots-Irish ancestors. A native Texan, she has lived in Oklahoma and for short times Oregon. As a mortgage loan underwriter she traveled the country and was able to see forty-three states, including many of the places she writes about. She lives in Shamrock, Texas with two chocolate labs and her extensive history book collection which she obtained while traveling.